SAMSON

NO ORDINARY SUPERHERO

Betty Collins Smith

WESTBOW
PRESS®
A DIVISION OF THOMAS NELSON
& ZONDERVAN

Scripture taken from the King James Version of the Bible.

This is a work of fiction. All of the characters, names, incidents, organizations, and dialogue in this novel are either the products of the author's imagination or are used fictitiously.

WestBow Press books may be ordered through booksellers or by contacting:

WestBow Press
A Division of Thomas Nelson & Zondervan
1663 Liberty Drive
Bloomington, IN 47403
www.westbowpress.com
1 (866) 928-1240

ISBN: 978-1-9736-4140-7 (sc)
ISBN: 978-1-9736-4139-1 (hc)
ISBN: 978-1-9736-4141-4 (e)

Library of Congress Control Number: 2018911666

Print information available on the last page.

WestBow Press rev. date: 10/25/2018

Dedicated to my Lord and Savior Jesus Christ for putting this story in my heart.

To my beautiful granddaughter, Jordan Shular. Jordan was only twelve years old when I started writing this book with three others. I allowed her to read several pages of it then. My goal was to inspire her to read more. She became so excited and told me that she liked *Samson* better than my first book, *The Rise of TEHH, Thomas Edison Hamilton Hancock*. Several years later, she reminded me that she was waiting on me to publish her book.

To my niece and her husband, Monique and Jimmy McNeily. I accidentally omitted their names in my first book.

And to all my family and friends.

In loving memory of my loving husband,
Reverend Morgan A. Smith
August 3, 2017

CONTENTS

CONTENTS

CHAPTER 1

Who is this Samson?

And Samson called unto the LORD, and said, O Lord GOD, remember me, I pray thee, and strengthen me, I pray thee, only this once, O God, that I may be at once avenged of the Philistines for my two eyes.

—Judges 16:28

IT'S NOT EVERY DAY THAT A BOY GETS TO EXPERIENCE life with a real Bible hero, but I did. I still find it hard to imagine all the things that happened to me. My name is Samson Avery. This is my story of how a real Bible character helped me become no ordinary superhero.

I was just an average boy living on a farm in Soyerville, Texas, usually getting in trouble—until I read a story in the Bible. It all started with me wanting to know why my mother gave me this name. I heard someone calling Samson one day and thought they were calling me. How embarrassing it was when I discovered they were calling their mule. Most people around here didn't name their children Samson, just their animals. There are five Samsons around these parts: a dog, a mule, a horse, a bull, and me. I was curious to learn why she named me Samson. I thought this was probably the cause of all my problems. I decided to ask her about it.

Knowing I was going to get one of my mother's long sermons, I simply prepared myself to listen.

She looked at me with that intriguing smile of hers and said, "I named you after the Samson in the Bible. I always loved reading about him. You see, he was one of the judges of Israel. He was not just a judge but also the strongest man in the Bible." Then she smiled and said, "I believe he was a good-looking man too."

I liked the "good-looking man" part. Then she said something I didn't expect.

"His life story inspired me a lot. But, I tell you as your mother, be careful who you trust in this life. I sure don't want you to experience any of the things he did."

Now that part I couldn't understand because I didn't even know this man. She told me she read the story to me many times when she was pregnant with me.

Smiling, she said, "You would just move inside me like you enjoyed hearing me read to you. That was the reason I named you Samson. Honey, your name has nothing to do with you getting in trouble. Believe me when I tell you, that's your very own doing."

One evening after school, I decided I wanted to read about this so-called Samson for myself. I boldly went into the house, put my books on the table, and yelled at the top of my voice, "Mama, where is the book about Samson?"

Yelling back, she said, "On the table by my bed. Why do you want to know?"

"I want to read about him!" I yelled back.

Suddenly, I heard glass breaking in the kitchen and rushed in to see what happened.

"Mama, is everything okay?"

She looked at me and said, "Yes, but I have never known you to ask to read the Bible in all your sixteen years. Are you okay?"

"Yes, Mama. I'm fine."

She had dropped several of her favorite plates. I cleaned up the broken glass, got the Bible, and went outside to read it. I found a comfortable spot and began searching the Bible. Having exhausted myself, I still couldn't find the Book of Samson anywhere.

"Mama," I yelled, "Where's the Book of Samson in the Bible?"

I knew deep down in my heart this was going to make her day, and I would never hear the end of it. She knew exactly where it was. Mama was a great Bible teacher. People would call her and ask her questions about the Bible. Amazingly, she would always know the answer. She told me God had given her a special gift to help people understand the Bible.

She opened the back door with a great big smile on her face that resonated with a silent *hallelujah* and said, "There's no such book as the Book of Samson in the Bible, sugar."

Shocked when she said that, I asked, "Why not, Mama?"

"Now, don't you ruffle your feathers," she said. "You can find his story in the Book of Judges."

Already frustrated from searching through the Bible, I asked, "Where 'bout in Judges, Mama?"

She knew I was a little frustrated and smiled. She said, "Start at the thirteenth chapter, and read to the end of the story. You'll know when you get there."

"Thanks Mama," I said.

I felt so relieved when I found it. She smiled and went back into the house. Suddenly, she started beating her tambourine and singing really loud, like she does in church when someone gets religion.

CHAPTER 2

Discovering Samson

I MUST ADMIT, I DIDN'T LIKE TO READ THAT MUCH. I just did what I had to do in school and nothing more. However, this Samson obsession was getting the best of me. He stays on my mind, and I'm determined to find out why.

I sat there in the backyard under the big oak tree, enjoying the breeze. I started reading about him and soon fell asleep. I didn't realize I was asleep until Mama woke me up to eat dinner. Eagerly, I stood up, and the Bible fell to the ground.

As usual, she quickly overreacted by saying, "Go right now and put it back on my table."

"I'm sorry, Mama," I said. "I didn't mean to drop it."

I honestly wanted to finish reading the story later.

Groggy, I followed her into the kitchen. As usual, I sat down at the table knowing exactly what she would say.

"Samson," she said, "get up from there and go wash your hands. Why do I have to tell you the same thing every day? I just don't understand."

Grinning, I went to wash my hands, and quickly returned to the table and started eating my dinner.

"Mama, you outdid yourself this time. Dinner was delicious," I told her after we finished eating.

Getting up from the table, she said, "Thank you, sugar," and took my plate and placed it in the sink.

Mama cooked a good dinner that day. Daddy had gotten her a new stove, and she wanted to see if it cooked as well as her old one did. She was pleased with that new stove, and so was I.

While putting the rest of the dishes in the sink, she said, "Oh, by the way Samson, your daddy will be in a little later tonight. He had to take care of some business in town. It's board meeting time, and his good friend, the mayor, is going to be there. He told me to tell you that your package arrived today. Have all your chores done. He'll help you put it together when he gets home."

I was so excited that Daddy had gotten me the pedal boxcar I wanted. I just couldn't sit still. Having him help me put it together was my greatest motivation in getting one. Now, all I wanted to do was win a race and make him proud of me.

Daddy is a wonderful man. He takes great care of Mama and me. Mama loves him with all her heart. There's nothing he wouldn't do to please her.

What makes my daddy so extraordinary is that he's short in stature. He's just a little over five foot three. The average height for men in Soyerville is five foot eight. After people talk to him on the telephone, they are always amazed when they see him in person. However, that deep voice of his always puts their minds at ease. He's simply the smartest man I know.

Mama loves him with all her heart, and she's not ashamed to show it. There's nothing she wouldn't do to please him.

Now, my daddy loves me too, even though I get in lots of trouble. He would say, "Samson, look at you. You're already taller than me and still growing. I expect you'll probably be one of the tallest boys in Soyerville." He said I would be tall like his granddaddy, who was over six feet tall. Daddy inherited his height from his grandmother.

One day, while Daddy and I were fishing down at the creek, he told me that I was not a bad boy, but a curious one like he was. He said when he was a boy, trouble was his best friend too. He said he loved to raid the neighbors' watermelon patches and fruit trees. That made me feel good. However, I never would have thought Daddy got into any trouble the way he would whip me.

One time, Daddy got to fighting with some bees. He tried to steal their honey and lost the battle. His daddy said he didn't need a whipping that day because the bees had done it for him. Daddy told me, "No matter what, stay away from those bees." Even with a swollen face, he still had to go to school.

Sometimes, the bullies around Soyerville would tease me about my daddy. They wanted to know if he was my real daddy since I was so much taller than him. That made me so angry. I wanted to tie them all in knots the way Samson did the foxes' tails, when his father-in-law gave his wife to another man to marry.

Besides our height, Daddy and I look just alike. I have his eyes, nose, and mouth. I wish I had gotten his brains; then I would do much better in school. Math is my hardest subject, but Daddy comes to my rescue when he sees me struggling with it.

Later that night after dinner, I went to bed and couldn't sleep because I had to read more about Samson. I read a few chapters and began to like him a lot. He was a strong man with long hair and loved to tell riddles. I bet he was handsome, just like Mama said, and all the young women loved him.

I don't know when I fell asleep, but I woke up with the book still in my hands and on the same page. I had never done that before. I'm a real tosser and turner in bed.

Staggering into the shower, I turned on the water and woke up. Enjoying the water beating down on my body, I thought about Samson. Excitedly, I began to shake the water from my hair. Smiling, I tried to flex what few muscles I had. I took a towel and wrapped it around my waist real tight, admiring myself in the mirror. I was trying to imagine Samson as a boy my age.

Suddenly, Mama knocked on the door, shattering all my thoughts, saying, "Samson, breakfast is ready. Hurry up so you won't miss your bus."

"Okay, Mama," I said.

I quickly put on my clothes, ate as fast as I could, and ran out to meet the bus. That old yellow bus slowly came up the road with a trail of dust following behind it. The bumpy road made the bus rock from side to side.

Mr. Joshua is our bus driver. He gets up with the chickens and is never late. We all respect him because he looks out for us and loves to give advice. One day while on the bus, he told us that he once served in the military. He said he often has flashbacks. When he's alone on the bus, he hears gunfire. Sometimes, the fields would remind him of Vietnam. On that day, he begged us to be quiet because all the noise could possibly push him over the edge. He didn't want to do something bizarre while we were on the bus. We have the quietest bus in all of Soyerville.

The day Mr. Joshua told us this, I went home and told my daddy what he said. Daddy quickly reminded me that I better not give him any trouble, unless I wanted something on my behind. That's one of the reasons why I don't bother him. My daddy didn't play with that belt. It makes me hurt just to think about it.

The bus finally made its way to my stop, and the door opened.

"Good morning, Mr. Joshua," I said as I got on the bus.

"Good morning, Samson. You sure are getting taller these days. What's your mama feeding you, son?"

"Everything, Mr. Joshua. Everything," I said, and took my seat.

There were four other kids on the bus. That was great because it meant the bus was extremely quiet. We had about twenty-five minutes before the next stop. Some were catching up on their homework, but I decided to catch up on my sleep.

It wasn't long before I began dreaming about Samson. I saw him take a lion and kill it with his bare hands like it was nothing. I saw him fight off an army of men with the jawbone of a donkey. I couldn't believe it. *No way can one man fight off so many men,* I thought.

I called to him and said, "Hey, Samson. I sure wish

I could be just like you. Then the kids wouldn't pick on me all the time."

Samson quickly stopped what he was doing, looked my way, and started coming toward me. I was startled! It seemed as if he knew me and had been waiting for me. His large hand reached out and touched me. I felt the touch, but then, there was also this strange shake.

Then I heard someone say, "Samson, wake up."

I slowly opened my eyes and almost jumped out of my skin. It wasn't Samson at all. It was Moose. He really scared me. He interrupted the dream of my life. Now I will never know what Samson was going to do. I wanted to strangle Moose for messing up my dream.

Jimmy Beaverton was Moose's real name. To see him, anyone would know why we called him Moose. He was the largest kid in school, but gentle in nature.

Moose moved from the back of the bus to sit by me and asked, "Samson, are you okay? I heard you talking in your sleep. I thought something was wrong with you. I have never heard you do that before."

Yawning, I said, "Me? I was talking in my sleep?"

He said, smiling, "Yeah! Tell me, Samson, what were you dreaming about? It seemed like it was a good dream. Was it about a girl? I bet it was about a girl, wasn't it?"

I sat up, yawned, and stretched some more. Still kind of groggy, I said, "Yeah," to shut him up.

He said enthusiastically, "I knew it was about a girl. I just knew it!"

The bus finally slowed down and stopped. Mr. Joshua opened the door to let all the other kids on and drove us to school. I was still thinking about Samson when we got there. I just couldn't seem to shake the thought of him.

CHAPTER 3

Delilah, My Love

And it came to pass afterward, that he loved a woman in the valley of Sorek, whose name was Delilah.

—Judges 16:4

THE SCHOOL BELL RANG, AND WE ALL WENT INSIDE. I felt someone pat me on the back but thought nothing of it. A lot of kids were going through the door at that time.

As I headed toward my locker, Josh, Rooster, and Kevin cornered me. They were trying to take my lunch and what change I had in my pockets. They always tried to take our lunch money or anything they thought was valuable.

While we were tussling in the hallway like we were playing football or something, one of the teachers heard all the commotion. He came out of his classroom and said, "Break it up! Get to your classes right now!" We all took off running down the hall.

That was perfect timing. I knew I couldn't beat the three of them alone. How I wished I was Samson at that time.

All out of breath, I put my books in my locker. Then I quickly went to my class and took a seat.

Amazingly, out of the clear blue, Cynthia Jackson passed me a note. I couldn't believe it. *My sweet Delilah noticed me and sent me a note. Wow,* I thought. She was so cute, and secretly, I liked her a lot.

I slowly opened the note and read it. *"Samson, someone put a bad note on your back. Hurry and take it off before the teacher sees it."*

I reached for the note on my back, and there it was. I quickly took it off and read it before the teacher came by. *"Kick me! I'm so easy,"* it said in big black letters. Seriously, I felt humiliated. No wonder everyone laughed as I walked down the hall. I looked back at that beautiful face and mouthed, "Thank you."

While thinking about the note, a rush of anger came over me, but I didn't show it. I wondered who had played a dirty trick like that on me. For the rest of the day, I thought about the person who put that note on my back. I also wondered what Samson would have done in a situation like that. He certainly wouldn't have taken that from anyone. He probably would have torn that person and the whole school apart.

When I got home from school, I found Mama had cooked another good dinner. We could all smell it in the air on the bus. We were held hostage by the smell.

Mr. Joshua rubbed his stomach and said, "Lord have mercy. That really smells good. What's your mama cooking today, Samson?"

"I really don't know, Mr. Joshua," I said. "It's always a surprise to me."

All the kids said their stomachs were growling while they talked about how good the food smelled.

When the door opened, I got off the bus. They all yelled, "Throw us a chicken bone or something, Samson. We are so hungry. Bye, Samson!" The bus pulled off, and I could hear Mr. Joshua telling the kids to quiet down as I went into the house.

Inside, I noticed Mama was setting the table for dinner. Amazingly, I went straight to the bathroom and washed my hands without thinking.

As I sat down at the table, Mama said, "Samson, get up from there and go—" But, she quickly stopped that sentence like she was putting on brakes. Then she asked, "Did you just wash your hands?"

I smiled and said, "Yes, ma'am. I sure did."

Mama seemed shocked. She came over and felt my

forehead to make sure I was all right. She looked up and said, "Thank you, Lord."

While I was putting the food on my plate, I said, "Mama, I really like the story about Samson. I sure wish I could be just like him."

She smiled and said, "Boy, that's too much power for you. The way you get into trouble, you would destroy this whole town in no time. Baby, I love you the way you are."

She told me to hurry up and eat my dinner so I could finish my chores before it got too late. Then she went into the sitting room to relax.

After I finished my chores, I said, "Mama, is it okay for me to go down by the creek and read the Bible?"

She smiled and said, "It's okay, but bring it back in a little while because I want to read it later."

I was so excited and took off running with the Bible in my hand. When I reached the creek, I found a spot under a nice shade tree and began to read about Samson. I sat there, wondering how he came up with those riddles the way he did. He really had a lot of people scratching their heads.

Suddenly, something strange began to happen to me. When I looked up from the pages of the book, things around me began to distort. I didn't know what to do. It seemed as if Samson was calling out to me from the pages of the Bible.

"Samson, come here," he said as his voice rumbled.

That voice caused even more distortion in the things around me. Everything was changing. It was too late for me to run. Somehow, I was becoming part of his world. Sitting there, in an instant, I was transported to his time. It was the time of Bible days.

I felt really scared. Looking around, I realized this was a place I had never seen before in my life. It showed no likeness to the time in which I lived. I could hear people talking behind me. Slowly, I turned to see what was happening. There, standing amid the crowd, was this giant of a man towering over everyone. I was in awe of this man. He had to be the mighty Samson. I stood there, looking up at him. He was everything the Bible said he was and more. He had very long hair. He had muscles everywhere; he was indeed very strong, and a very good-looking man at that. I couldn't believe my eyes. I had to touch him and his clothes to make sure he was real.

He looked down at me, smiled, and said, "I'm as real as they come. Follow me."

After that, I felt compelled to see where this journey would lead.

"Now tell me about those kids who beat you up all the time," he said, smiling as we walked along.

Frowning, I couldn't believe he heard what I said. I was speechless.

"It's okay," he said. "Don't worry. I'll teach you how to take care of yourself one day." He posed no real threat to me. It was as if I was with a big brother.

Following him was so real. I could smell the dust as we walked along the dusty roads. I saw the people who lived in fear of him. I saw the people who were glad to see him waving and shouting his name when he showed me his hometown of Zorah.

"This is the place where I was born." He looked at me and said, "Can I call you Little Sam?"

I was amazed again that he knew my name and said, "You know my name?"

He laughed and said, "Of course I know your name. You were named after me, Samson."

I smiled and said, "Yes, sir. Call me, Little Sam."

He said, "Little Sam, that's my parents' house ahead. My father's name was Manoah. I tell you, I had some great times growing up there. My parents were descendants of Dan, father of the Danites. He was the son of Jacob by Rachel's maidservant Bilhah. We were called the Danites."

Suddenly, I remembered hearing my mama talking to some people about the Danites. I didn't know she was really talking about Samson's folks.

He said, "My mother was very old and had never had children. She told me that an angel of God appeared to her one day. He told her that she would have a son, and that son would begin to deliver Israel out of the hands of the Philistines. That son was me. She called me her miracle baby. I grew bigger and stronger than all the other children. Naturally, they looked to me to protect them. Little Sam, you don't have to worry when you are with me. I will always protect you."

Miraculously, I had become part of his world. I didn't know if I would ever get to return home. It was so strange, but fascinating at the same time. I felt the earth shake as he jumped from rocks and small cliffs. I could even feel the water as I crossed the creeks and streams with him. I could feel my own hair blowing in the wind.

I was bending over, trying to catch a fish, when I heard my mama calling me. I slowly came to myself as if I was coming out of a trance. Everything around me was back to normal. I closed the book, jumped up, and went to see what she wanted.

"Samson," she said, "don't you know you have been sitting in that one spot reading for two hours? Baby, you have never sat still that long for anything. Are you all right?"

"I'm fine, Mama. There is nothing wrong with me. I was just enjoying reading about Samson," I said.

"Thank you, Lord. I never thought I would ever see this day," she said, smiling.

The next day, we got out of school early. I hurried into the house, washed up, ate my dinner, and did my chores. Then I asked Mama if I could read her Bible again.

She said, "I'm so proud of you for reading, but I'm getting kind of jealous of Samson because he's taking you away from me."

She said the story wasn't that long and I could have finished it in a couple of hours. She wondered if I was having trouble with my reading since it was taking me so long to finish it.

I politely said, "Mama, I'm trying to memorize the whole story just like it's written in the Bible. I want to be able to recite it or teach in church for you one day when I'm older."

She raised up, smiled, and said, "Honey, that is so wonderful. Go on so you can hurry and get back here."

I went on down by the creek, sat under that same old tree, and started reading about Samson. I was excited to see where we would go today.

Suddenly, I was lost in his world. He began telling me all about his God.

He said, "Little Sam, I want you to know that my God is the true and living God who lives in heaven. He is the one who made the heaven and the earth and everything that's in it. He is the one true God. He is the one who gave me all my power and strength. You see, when the Spirit of the Lord comes upon me, I become a human weapon for the Lord to destroy the Philistines.

They controlled my people for forty years. In obedience to God, there was one thing I was to never do."

Eagerly, I said, "What was that, Samson?"

He said sadly, "I was to never take a razor to my head."

"A razor?" Puzzled, I asked, "What do you mean by that?"

He looked at me as if I should have known what he was talking about and said, "I was to never cut my hair or have it cut. You see, I would lose all my strength and power. I would become as weak as any ordinary man."

I found it hard to believe that his strength and power was in all those long black locks of hair on his head. I couldn't help but touch my own hair.

We sat on a large rock by a stream. He told me some of the other things that had happened to him, including the story of how some of his so-called friends got his wife to betray him by revealing his riddles.

His wife was a beautiful Philistine, but he said she was very weak. Even though his parents didn't want him to marry her, but an Israelite instead, they honored his request. They went with him to a place called Timnath, which was a Philistine city in Canaan. He said the Philistines had dominion over Israel then. He wanted to ask this woman to marry him because she pleased him.

While they were on their way to Timnath, he said he

came to the vineyards there and a young lion tried to kill him. He stood up and told me very enthusiastically, "The power of my God came upon me, and I killed that lion with my bare hands, Little Sam. I never told this to my parents. It probably would have scared them to death."

I was spellbound as he spoke, trying to imagine myself doing the same thing. He was so animated, and the best teacher I had ever known.

Then he said, "When it came time for me to go get my wife and bring her home with me, I passed by the place where I had killed the lion. I looked, and his carcass was still there. To my surprise, a swarm of bees were making delicious honey in the carcass of that lion."

I said seriously, "You mean dead bones, right?"

He laughed and said, "Yeah, dead bones! I just couldn't resist it, Little Sam. I took a handful of that honey and ate it."

I remembered he had said he wasn't supposed to touch unclean things because he was a Nazirite unto God, but he did it anyway.

He said, "Little Sam, I tell you, that was some of the best honey I had ever eaten."

I just knew God must have struck him with lightning or something after that. So, I asked him, "What happened?"

He smiled and said, laughing, "Absolutely nothing, and I gave some to my mother and father. Now, let's go."

As we walked, I felt mesmerized listening to him. I couldn't believe he gave his parents some of that forbidden honey. They probably would have died, knowing what he did.

He wanted to finish the story about his wife and the riddle. He said, "I told my wife a riddle that no one in this world would have been able to guess. Thirty sheets and thirty changes of garments were riding on that riddle."

He was getting angrier by the minute as he continued to tell me the story. "The woman kept nagging me about it. So, I told her my secret to the riddle because I couldn't take any more. She had gotten on my last nerve. I didn't think she would ever tell anyone."

He stood up and yelled at the top of his voice as the ground shook. "She told them my riddle! No way could they have known!"

The way he moved his hands was making me a little scared. He had lost the bet, and he didn't like to lose. The riddle was about the honey he had found in the lion's carcass. His story was getting so interesting that I didn't want it to end.

Strangely enough, I heard my mama calling me again. I couldn't understand why. I hadn't been there but a few minutes. She interrupted another great story. I slowly got up and went to see what she wanted.

She put her hands on her hips and said, "Did you know that you have been sitting in that one spot reading for two and a half hours this time?"

"Two and a half hours, Mama?" I said. I couldn't believe it.

"Honey, for two and a half hours," she said, smiling. "Trouble has been able to take a nap for the first time in your life."

"Mama," I said, "I can see why you said Samson was so inspiring. He's really inspiring me."

She smiled and said, "Baby, you now wash your hands without me telling you. That's inspiration enough for me. Thank you so much, Samson!"

"You're welcome, Mama," I said.

She quickly said, "Not you, boy—Samson in the Bible."

She asked for her Bible because it was her quiet time and she was ready to read it.

CHAPTER 4

A Life-Changing Experience

THE WORLD HAD HAD TWO AND A HALF HOURS OF peace, and all my chores were done. I guess it was time for me to go and wake up trouble before it got too late. I decided I would go over to the other side of the creek. I saw some of the kids swimming and playing over there.

First, I just had to tease Mr. Grayson's hunting dogs he kept behind the fence. Mr. Grayson is one of our neighbors who sells pigs for a living. His house is on the way to the creek. Somehow, those dogs knew when I was around.

I saw my little friend Stinky the skunk I had charmed to come to me. I hoped it was him, because all skunks look alike. As he came closer, I prayed he wouldn't spray me with skunk pee. I picked him up, rubbed his back as always, and dropped him in the pen with the dogs.

When those dogs saw Stinky, fear came all over them. They tried with all they had to get out of that pen. Stinky got scared and began spraying them with skunk pee. Every time a dog would try to get close to Stinky, he would let them have it again. They were barking and jumping around, trying to get that stuff out of their eyes. Those were some stinky dogs. They did all kinds of flips. I couldn't stop laughing because they were so funny.

Mr. Grayson suddenly came out the door to see what was going on with his dogs. I hid behind the shed so he wouldn't see me.

"Mary, a skunk done got in the pen with my dogs. Good gracious," he said.

He walked over to his dogs holding his nose. "It smells awful bad out here. How did that skunk get in my pen? You can't stay in there," he said.

I was laughing so hard my stomach hurt.

Unexpectedly, he yelled, "Samson, are you 'round here boy? This got your name written all over it!"

That's when I took off laughing and running before he saw me. That was so much fun.

I laughed that off and headed on down to the creek. I saw a beehive hanging from a tree in the distance. I just couldn't resist it. I thought about what my daddy told me about those bees, but I just had to see for myself.

The hive was so full of honey that it was dripping to the ground. I thought about Samson and decided to taste it. My goodness, it was so good. I knew my mama would love to have some of that honey.

I picked up a big stick and threw it at the beehive, trying to knock it down. The stick hit the hive, but it didn't come down. Those bees got a whiff of me, and they all came flying in my direction. I had to run for my life fighting off bees. The only place I thought I would be safe was in the creek. I was praying I wouldn't drown.

I jumped into the water and held my breath until I thought the bees were gone. When I raised my head to see if they were gone, several of them stung me on the forehead again. I got some bad stings, but nothing like my daddy had in his day.

After the battle with the bees, I went on down to the other side of the creek. I was hoping to get a glimpse of Cynthia again if she was there. Most of the kids hung out there so they could swim and play games. I just wanted to see Cynthia. If I was Samson, she would be the one I would tell all my secrets to.

I sneaked over, hiding behind some bushes to see what was going on. The last time I had gone over to be with them, some of the guys jumped on me and beat me up. I had a busted lip and a knot on my head for days.

I peeped and didn't see Cynthia, but I saw my enemies: Jason, Eric, and Almond. They were teasing little Rodney Johnson. They were trying to throw him in the creek. Rodney couldn't swim. They terrified him by making him think they were going to throw him in. He hollered for dear life, but there was nothing I could do to help him. They grabbed him by the arms and legs and swung him to the edge of the creek bank, pulled him back, and let him fall to the ground. He was so scared. He got up crying and eventually went home. I felt sorry for him.

After that, Jason, Eric, and Almond started throwing rocks into the creek and looking for their next victim. They made me so angry that I decided to leave and go home too. That was one time I wished I was big enough to beat them all down with a passion!

I slowly crawled away, hoping they didn't see me. When I thought I had gotten away, I heard Jason yell, "There he is! Let's get Samson!"

They all took off running after me. I ran with all my might, trying to get away from them. I knew they would hurt me if I was caught. I prayed for the day when I wouldn't have to run from anyone any more.

I heard Jason tell some of the boys, "Go the other way and cut him off."

I was running with all I had, dodging trees and bushes, jumping over little streams and rocks, kind of like Samson. I was so scared and tired. I could feel my heart pounding in my chest, and I was raining sweat. Suddenly, I tripped over something and fell to the ground and hit my head on a rock. I could hear voices, but I couldn't see anyone. I tried to get up, but I couldn't move. I must have fallen asleep.

It was a few hours later when I finally woke up and noticed that I was in a strange place. As I began to focus, I saw Mama reading her Bible and Daddy taking a nap in the corner.

I called to her and said, "Mama, what are we having for dinner?"

Strangely, Mama turned in my direction and said, "Samson! Oh my Lord!" She saw that I was awake and strangely started screaming, "Nurse! Nurse, he's awake. Samson is awake!"

Daddy jumped up from his chair and rushed over to see me with tears in his eyes. "Samson! Son, you are awake. Thank God!"

Everyone came rushing into the room to see me. I didn't know what was going on. Doctors eagerly rushed in to examine me. They were amazed and said things looked exceptionally good. Everybody was so happy. Daddy was still crying. I had never seen him cry before.

Mama wiped her eyes and said, "Samson, you have been in this hospital in a coma for over three months."

I was shocked and said, "For three months, Mama?"

I didn't know I was in the hospital or that I had been in a coma. I thought I was at home in my own bed. I just couldn't believe it.

They all said I had really changed. My hair had grown longer. I had gotten taller and muscular. Doctors couldn't understand what was going on with me. Everything should have been the opposite of what happened. A doctor finally said that even though I was in a coma, my brain waves were very active. In fact, more active than usual. It was as if I was talking to someone the whole time I was in the hospital.

Mama said it was a miracle. That was one of the happiest days of my parents' lives, when my eyes opened and they heard my voice.

"Mama," I said, "I'm so hungry I could eat a horse right now."

She smiled and said, "Sugar, I don't think you will be eating a horse today."

I was so excited I couldn't wait when the nurse brought me a covered plate. I had many things going through my mind. But when Mama removed the lid, I saw the plate only featured some gelatin and juice. I became sick all over again. I was hoping for some fried chicken and my favorite caramel cake. However, I quickly ate the gelatin and asked for more. I was just that hungry.

That evening, some more doctors came into my room.

They told Mama and Daddy they wanted to watch me a few more weeks to make sure that everything continued to improve. They wanted to get me eating and walking before they allowed me to go home. One of the doctors told them my system wasn't strong enough just yet to tolerate solid foods, even if I thought it was. That didn't stop my hunger pangs at all. My stomach rumbled like a drum.

I begged, "Doctor, please, can I get something better to eat? I'm still very hungry."

The doctor smiled and said, "I understand. I'll have them add a few peaches to your gelatin and bring you a larger cup of delicious chicken broth," and he left.

CHAPTER 5

Samson is Changing Me

And Samson said unto them, Though ye
have done this, yet will I be avenged of you,
and after that I will cease.

—Judges 15:7

THE DAY CAME THAT THE DOCTORS FINALLY
released me from the hospital. Daddy was so excited
when he came to pick me up. He was so thankful that I
was finally coming home.

"Samson, you just don't know how much your mama
and I missed you."

He gave me a big hug that I will always remember.
The thing is I couldn't remember being away from them
but for a few hours.

"You are looking better than anyone could have ever

imagined. To think of what you've been through ... I thank God for bringing you back home to us," he said as he helped me into the truck.

As we drove off, I said, "How come Mama didn't come with you to get me, Daddy?"

"She stayed home because she wanted to make you a very special surprise."

When we got close to home, we found that Mama had cooked a good dinner, as usual. We could smell it coming up the road. This time, she had made my favorite caramel cake. That was my surprise. I like my caramel cake when it's warm.

Daddy had to help me around the house for a while. I was still weak and needed some assistance. However, I could feel myself getting stronger every day. It didn't take me long to learn how to walk again on my own after lying in bed for over three months.

One evening, I got up and slowly walked into the bathroom without any assistance and washed my hands. Then I made it to the table and sat down to eat dinner.

Mama looked at me with tears in her eyes, saying, "You did it! You did it all by yourself. Thank you, Lord."

"I told you, you were going to get out of that bed. Trouble has been very lonesome without you," Daddy said.

The truth was I smelled the food. That was the real motivator. Trouble had nothing to do with it. I took one look at the food on the table and started eating like I was crazy.

"Slow down, son," Daddy said. "You're going to hurt yourself. You act like you're starving or something."

Daddy just didn't know. I *was* starving. That food was so good I couldn't help myself.

"Mama," I said, eating, "you outdid yourself again this time!"

"Well, thank you. I missed hearing that when you were in the hospital."

She had a great big smile on her face as tears ran from her eyes. I ate all I could and then went outside and sat on the porch to allow my food to digest.

Later, Mama came out and said, "You need to go to bed and get your rest now—doctor's orders."

While I was resting in bed, I guess I slowly drifted off to sleep. I heard someone calling me, and I said, "Huh?"

He said, "How are you feeling, Little Sam?"

I said, "Okay."

I turned to see who it was. It was Samson coming toward me. I was so glad to see him.

"I came back to check on you," he said.

Overjoyed, I said, "You sure did. Thank you so much."

He smiled, flexed his muscles, and said, "Come on now! It's time for your exercise. You have to keep up your strength and stay in shape."

Strangely, he said, "You just might have to fight some low-down, dirty Philistines one day."

Those were the people of his day. I couldn't understand why he would say something like that.

Then he said, "The spirit of the Philistines will always be around. They were the oppressors who enslaved my people of Israel, and they will do the same thing to you and your people. They will take your land and your life. Some you will come to love, and others you will come to hate. Always keep your eyes and ears open, Little Sam—always."

He took a deep breath and started running and yelling at me. "Come on, Little Sam! Follow me, and try to keep up this time."

I took off running after him. I didn't know where we were going, but we ran for hours, leaping over rocks and creeks, and going up and down hills. Eventually, we came to a place where there were a lot of huge rocks, and he showed me how to throw them.

"Pick up one, Little Sam, and focus," he said. "These rocks will help make you even stronger."

I began picking up those big rocks and throwing them. I even picked up giant boulders like they were nothing. That was awesome.

"Very good, Little Sam. Now catch this one," he said.

He began throwing those huge rocks to me, saying, "Catch it! You sure don't want one of these to fall on you. Muscle up now!"

When I saw that big boulder coming at me, I muscled up all the strength I had and caught it. I was amazed at myself. He patted me on the back and told me that I had done a great job. He then decided we needed to rest awhile after a workout like that.

We were sitting around the fire, eating fish, and talking about his life when someone shook me and said, "Samson, wake up. It's time to take your medicine."

My eyes slowly opened. I felt strange because I thought I was already awake. It was Mama. I looked around and saw no mountains, no lake, no fish, and no Samson. I was still in my bed. I had only been dreaming, but it all seemed so real to me.

Mama wondered why I was acting strangely and said, "Samson, are you okay?"

Somewhere between sleeping and waking, I told her that I was fine. However, she noticed that I was soaking wet with sweat and my bed was too. She asked me to get up and put on some dry clothes and take my medicine. She would change my bed. She thought I had a very high fever.

I changed my clothes, took my medicine, and went to sit with Daddy in the other room while she changed my bed. I was afraid to go back to sleep after that. That was a life-changing experience.

Am I going crazy or what? I thought. I was so confused.

CHAPTER 6

Realizing My Own Strength

A MONTH OR SO LATER, I FELT MUCH STRONGER, and Mama allowed me to go out in the backyard for a while alone. I sat under the big oak tree.

Everything looked so strange to me. Because I had grown a lot, everything seemed so much smaller. I stood up by that big oak tree to see just how much I had grown. I had a habit of cutting my height into it with an old pocketknife I had found. I always hid it under a rock nearby.

It shocked me to see that I had grown over a foot in a few short months while in a coma. *This is just impossible,* I thought. I wanted to understand how something like this could have happened to me. At this rate, I would be a giant by the end of the year. I was really scared.

Suddenly, my head started hurting, and I sat down in a nearby chair.

Mama came outside to check on me and asked, "How are you feeling?"

"I'm okay, but my head is hurting a little," I said, looking down.

"Okay, let me go get your medicine, and I'll be right back," she said.

She went into the house to get my medicine and quickly returned. I took it, and she went back into the house.

I got up and sat in the swing. While sitting there, the strangest thing began to happen. My legs started swelling up. I couldn't understand what was happening. It was so scary. My pajama pant legs split open. I didn't know what to do. I got up and started walking around the outside of the house to ease the pain.

Oddly, I felt a pebble or something in my shoe. I stopped and leaned against a tree to take it out. Unexpectedly, the tree started leaning and fell. I had to brace myself and quickly step away to keep from falling with it. That big tree fell to the ground with a bang and scared the living daylights out of me. I could hear the roots tearing away from the ground when it happened. It wasn't a dream this time. It was terribly real. I was so glad the tree fell away from our house.

Mama heard the noise and came rushing out to

see what all the commotion was about. She started screaming, "Samson! Samson! Where are you? Are you okay?"

She grabbed me. She looked at that tree and said, "Oh my goodness! It came up from the root. Thank God you're okay."

All I could say was "I really don't know, Mama." I stood there in shock of what had happened.

She hugged me and said, "Come on in the house. You could have been killed out here. Thank you, Lord! Thank you."

I was truly in a state of confusion. I still don't know what happened. I simply leaned against a tree, and it fell. *That's utterly impossible for me or anyone to do. Only a superhuman like Samson can do stuff like that*, I thought.

I went into the house with Mama, went to bed, and soon fell asleep. It wasn't long before I heard Samson's voice.

"Great job, Little Sam. You are stronger than I thought. You brought that tree down with one hand. You've got to be careful when leaning against things at certain times. You can actually hurt someone."

I said, "What! Are you saying I did that?"

He smiled and said, "Well, it sure wasn't me."

He started running and laughing, saying, "Come on! Now keep up! You sure don't want the bears to get you around here."

"Bears!" I yelled while running to catch up with him.

We came to a river that had a waterfall nearby. It was a breathtaking sight. I had never seen anything like it before. While I was captivated by the water falling, he caught me off guard and threw me into the water.

I was so afraid. "I can't swim! Samson, please help me! I can't swim," I yelled.

He yelled back, "It's high time you learn. Now swim, Little Sam! You can do it!"

I tried with all I had to keep from drowning. I would sink down and try to come up again, but I couldn't. He jumped in and pulled me up. When I caught my breath, he just threw me back in again.

Angrily, he said, "Now swim, Little Sam! I'm going to do this all day until you learn!"

I was trying with all I had to catch my breath when I felt someone shaking me and calling my name.

"Samson! Samson wake up!"

Slowly opening my eyes, I saw it was only my daddy. I thought I was already awake. But it was a dream again. He asked me if I was okay because I was talking, tossing, and turning in my sleep. I was soaking wet with sweat again. Then he asked me about the tree in the backyard.

All I could say was "Daddy, it just fell."

He said, "Son, I'm so glad you didn't get hurt. Get up, change your clothes, and let's go eat dinner. Your mama did it again."

CHAPTER 7

Crazy as Those Foxes

A FEW MONTHS LATER WHILE SITTING UNDER THAT big oak tree, I remembered I used to read about Samson. I called Mama and asked her if I could read her Bible. It had been nearly five months since the last time I read it. I couldn't understand why Samson was always near me even though I wasn't reading about him.

Mama came out, put her hands on her hips, and looked at me strangely. "No, you can't have my Bible anymore," she said sharply.

I thought, *What did I do to make her say that?*

With a big smile on her face, she said, "You can't have mine because I got you your very own. Look under that pillow. It has your name on it."

I smiled and looked under the pillow, and there it was. I got up, gave her a big hug, and thanked her for my Bible.

"Now, don't you stay out here too long. You need your rest. I will be in the kitchen if you need me," she said.

Wow, my very own Bible with my name on it, I thought. I looked at that Bible and rubbed my fingers over my name written in big gold print—SAMSON. Then I held it close to my heart. *I have my very own Bible. Now I won't have to worry Mama about hers anymore,* I thought. Being in that coma was really starting to pay off. I saw her in the kitchen window and said, "I love you, Mama."

She said back, "I love you too, sugar," and she started singing her church song really loud.

I sat there in the backyard looking at the Bible for nearly a half hour before I decided to open it. What was I afraid of?

As I began to read about Samson, something strange began to happen to me, again. My head started hurting. This time, the pain was worse than ever. It was so bad I started crying and holding my head with my eyes closed. I began praying to Samson's God to help me. I felt like the whole world heard me scream out of my pain, but it didn't. I opened my eyes and saw only my mama through the kitchen window as the pain held me hostage. I know she would have heard me scream.

I closed my eyes and slowly opened them again. It was as if Samson's eyes became my eyes. My ears became his ears. My mouth became his mouth. As he moved, it was as if I was moving even though I wasn't moving. That feeling scared me so bad that I quickly closed the book. I was afraid to open it again.

There was no way I could tell Mama and Daddy what was happening to me. They would think I was going insane. I didn't know what to do.

Nervously, I picked up my Bible and started to go into the house to rest when I noticed the side of our house was leaning. It had dropped down into the ground. That tree did some major damage to the foundation when it fell. Now it was beginning to show. That was going to cost my daddy a lot of money to fix. Afraid he wasn't aware of it, I wanted to tell Mama so she could let him know about it.

Before I could do that, Samson came from out of nowhere. He went over, stooped down, and took a good look at the foundation of the house.

He said, "The foundation is sinking, Little Sam. That's very bad. That tree caused the foundation bricks to crack when the roots loosened the ground. They are now crumbling from the weight of the house, but I can fix it. You have any bricks around?"

Daddy always kept extra bricks nearby, and I showed him where they were. Samson picked up a big handful of bricks and laid them down by the foundation. Then he took some wood and broke it into the size he wanted with his bare hands. Amazingly, with one hand, he lifted the side of the house, with my mama in it, like it was nothing, placing a log under it with the other hand to hold it up. He made a mortar out of something and replaced all the bricks and wood without breaking a sweat. I couldn't believe it.

He got up, stood back and took a good look at his work, and said, "Now that's a lot better. It should last another fifty years. See you later, Little Sam," as he smiled and walked away.

When I stood up, my head started hurting again, but it suddenly stopped. Just like that, the pain was gone. I thought nothing else of what had happened since it was a dream that I was waking up from.

As I was going into the house, Mama met me at the door, saying, "I felt the house move. Did you feel anything? I know I'm not crazy."

"No, Mama," I said, "I didn't feel anything. I must have fallen asleep again."

"I guess it must have been a light earthquake or something," she said strangely.

I went into the house, thinking about what happened in the dream. I was still afraid to read my Bible. I quickly placed it under my mattress. However, I couldn't get the thought of Samson out of my head. *This can't be real*, I thought. Perhaps my medicine was affecting my mind.

That night, I would close my eyes and then wake up afraid to go back to sleep. Sometime during the night, I must have fallen asleep anyway. When I woke up, Samson was right there. I could see him in the mirror, sitting on my bed. I couldn't seem to shake him. It was like he was becoming me, or I was becoming him. I just didn't know.

Over time, I began to feel much better, and Mama noticed it. She decided she was not going to leave me at home another Sunday. She insisted that I go to church or else. Deep down in my heart, I felt this was not the day. I really didn't think I was ready for church so soon.

When we got there, everyone was glad to see me. We went in and took our seats. Mama seemed so proud to show me off to the congregation. I felt like one of her prized pies.

She turned, looked at me strangely, and said, "Samson, I am so glad the Lord blessed you to be here today. Do you think this would be a good time to give your life to the Lord?"

I was dumbfounded and swallowed my gum.

I said, "Mama, not yet. Let me think about it some more, please. I'm not quite well yet."

She whispered and said, "Don't you take too long now. The Lord has been too good to you."

Daddy leaned over and whispered to Mama, "Baby, leave the boy alone. When the time is right, he will break his neck going up there like I did."

"Thank you, Daddy," I said, smiling, and sat back in my seat to hear what the preacher was going to talk about.

I knew I should have stayed home. Of all the people in those sixty-six books of the Bible, the preacher chose to preach about Samson. His subject was love betrayed. I couldn't believe it. My head started spinning inside. I wanted to hurry out of there, but I couldn't. Deep down inside, I felt something terrible was about to happen. As he preached, I said to myself, *Please don't say her name. Please don't say her name.*

Mama looked at me and said, "What's wrong with you, Samson? Stop shaking like that."

That is exactly what the preacher did. He began talking about Delilah. My head started hurting a little, and I closed my eyes. The pain soon stopped.

When I opened my eyes, I could have died. I couldn't believe what I was seeing. Samson was up there on the pulpit. This giant of a man was standing up there, towering over the preacher. He was very upset. To be honest, Samson seemed madder than when his father-in-law gave his wife to another man and he set the foxes' tails on fire and burned up their fields. He was steaming mad.

What made it even hotter for me was he wanted to know why the preacher was talking about his woman.

He yelled, "Why is he talking about my woman, Little Sam? You better tell me right now before I skin this filthy, little Philistine alive."

His voice echoed throughout the building. He was

furious and ready to punch the preacher out. When I saw him making a fist, I knew I had to hurry and do something before he destroyed the church and the preacher.

The building started shaking a little but soon stopped. The preacher tried to calm the congregation and said, "Don't y'all worry. It's just a mild tremor."

That was no tremor. That was Samson getting ready to do some major damage.

I told Mama I had to go to the restroom and walked away. I rushed over to the door on the side where Samson was near the pulpit. I peeped in and called to him. "Samson! Hey, Samson!"

He turned and looked at me, saying, "What is it, Little Sam? Can't you see I'm busy?"

"Please come over here. I need to talk to you," I said.

"Let me finish this filthy, little Philistine off first. No one talks about my woman and live."

"He's not a filthy Philistine. He's our preacher. Please don't hurt him, Samson! Let him live, please," I begged.

I was pleading for the preacher's life very loudly. I had forgotten that no one could see or hear Samson, but everyone could certainly see and hear me. I had messed up big time.

The preacher stopped preaching. He looked in my direction, pointing for someone to take me out.

People were saying, "Please be quiet!" "Somebody please help take him out of here."

Ushers scrambled to take me out of the church. I felt like a common criminal. I had done the unthinkable. I had disrupted the services while the preacher was preaching and gravely embarrassed my parents. That was a no-no and almost punishable by death. I knew for certain that I would be on the Lord's bad list forever.

Mama and Daddy both jumped up out of their seats and came to see what was wrong with me. They thought I had gone crazy, considering what I had been through. Mama was steaming like Samson the bull. Samson, the one who caused me to get into all this trouble, stood there laughing at me. I had never been so embarrassed in my life. I didn't think I would be able to come back to this church ever again.

Mama grabbed me by the ear and took me out of the church, fussing at me. "If I had known you were going to embarrass us like this, I would have allowed you to stay home."

Daddy drove us straight home, trying to calm Mama down. Once at home, I went to my room, wishing I could crawl into a hole and never come out again. I wanted to die.

CHAPTER 8

Discovering Philistines

SEVERAL MONTHS LATER, MAMA AND DADDY drove into town to get groceries, and I stayed home alone for the first time since I had been sick. I was reading one of my comic books when my head started hurting. I took some medicine for it and went to bed.

I must have drifted off. I found myself dreaming about Samson, but I didn't see him this time. I heard a strange noise outside. I saw myself getting out of bed, putting on my clothes, and going outside to see what it was.

As I walked around the house, I met one of our neighbors' bulls. He had gotten out of his pasture. He was angry about something and snorting. He took one look at me and came charging after me. I ran with all I had. I had never been so scared.

Out of nowhere, Samson appeared to protect me. He jumped on that bull and hit him in the top of his head, and he fell to the ground. He came over and asked me if I was okay. That bull slowly staggered to his feet. Samson and I put him back in his pasture. He must have had a headache because he didn't give us any trouble.

I sat on an old log to catch my breath before I heard that strange noise again. I decided to walk on down by the North Creek side, where I heard cows and a truck. I thought it was my daddy selling off some of his cows. He did that every now and then.

When I reached the area, I realized it wasn't my daddy at all. It was some men stealing our cattle. That's how that bull got out. He was too much for them to handle, so they let him go. I hid behind some bushes and heard one of them say, "Hurry up, Joe. Let's get out of here. We have enough for now."

Then suddenly it happened. I saw Samson take a huge boulder and throw it at the truck. That boulder landed on the hood of that truck, smashing it into pieces. Those two men took off running like they had been struck by lightning. They were scared out of their senses. I stood there laughing at them running and falling and getting up again. *Why were they stealing our cattle? Who cleared this area and why?* I thought.

After that, I went back to the house, took off my clothes, got in bed, and went to sleep. I had a fantastic dream. Watching Samson in action made me want to be more and more like him.

A few days later, my daddy came into the house in the evening all out of breath. I heard Mama talking to him. She was trying to make sure he was okay.

I got out the bed, went in where they were, and said, "What's wrong, Daddy?"

"Someone has been stealing our cows and some of the neighbors' cows. We were out looking for them. I just can't understand what's going on here." He took a sip of his coffee and said, "We have never had this kind of problem before. How in the world are they getting our cattle out of the pastures without me or anyone knowing about it?"

When he said that, I remembered the dream I had a few days earlier. "Daddy," I said, "I thought they only did that back in cowboy days."

He said, "Son, they will still do it today if they can get away with it. We just don't know how they are doing it." He took a deep breath and said, "I have already lost twenty-five heads of cattle. If this keeps up, I won't have anything to sell."

They had checked around all the pasture areas and couldn't see how the crooks did it. There were no truck tracks or anything.

Amazingly, I said, "Daddy, did you check down by the North Creek side?"

He smiled and said, "No, we didn't check down there. It's too woody, and the brush is too thick. It would be impossible for the cows or anything to move about down there."

Then he said curiously, "Now, tell me why you asked me about the North Creek area."

I took a deep breath and said, "I had a dream about it. That's all."

He smiled and said, "You mean to tell me you had a dream about somebody stealing our cattle?"

"Yes, sir," I said. I told him about the two men down on the North Creek side who were loading a great big truck with our cows and a big rock fell on it.

He laughed and said, "That was really some kind of dream. I will go down there and check it out anyway." There was still a little light before dark, and he and the others could look around.

"Of all the places, I never would have thought to look down there in a million years," I heard him say as he went out the door smiling and shaking his head.

Everyone left to check out the North Creek area, including Mama. I was home alone.

Not long after they left, I felt very strange and my head started hurting. I became so hungry. I felt like I was starving. I felt like I had not eaten in weeks. I went into the kitchen to find something to eat. I looked in the refrigerator and found two big turkey legs. I quickly ate both. Then I ate half the chocolate cake Mama had made for Daddy and me. And I drank two big jars of milk. It all tasted so good, but for some strange reason, I was still hungry.

I saw two watermelons in the corner of the kitchen by the refrigerator and ate one of them. After that, I was satisfied. I let out a loud belch and felt great. Mama would have had a fit if she heard me do that.

Unexpectedly, my arms began swelling up, but I felt no pain. I decided to make a muscle in each of my arms and they blew up like balloons. I couldn't understand what was happening to me. I went into the bathroom and looked in the mirror. I lifted my shirt because my chest was swelling too. Amazingly, it began to look just like Samson's. I looked at my behind, and it was swelling and looking like Samson's too.

I yelled, "What in the world is happening to me?" Suddenly, I felt very dizzy. I laid across my bed and soon fell asleep.

When I woke up, I looked and felt normal. I was bored and decided to read a book. Of the few books I had, I felt compelled to read about Samson. I looked under my mattress, saw the Bible, and pulled it out, unsure of what to do. After the scare I got the last time I read it, I was still afraid. I slowly opened it, turning to the page where I left off reading. Nothing happened this time, so I began to read the story again.

I must have fallen asleep because I heard Mama calling me at the top of her voice. I had never heard her call me like that before. Instinctively, I thought, *Trouble. What have I done now?*

"Samson get in here, boy!" she said.

I jumped out of bed and went into the kitchen. My heart was beating ninety-nine miles a minute.

Nervously I asked, "What's wrong, Mama?"

Mama and Daddy were both standing by the refrigerator with the door wide open.

"What happened to my two turkey legs that were in here?" She was so angry with me.

"Mama, I was so hungry I ate them," I said sadly.

"Both of them?" They both asked.

"Yes," I said nervously.

She frowned and said, "Boy, there is no way you could have eaten two big turkey legs and a half a side of cake, drank nearly a gallon of milk, and ate a whole watermelon all by yourself. What's wrong with you? Who was in this house while we were away?"

"No one, Mama. I'm telling you the truth."

"You better be glad you are sick right now, because I could just skin you alive! Go to your room and think about this lie you just told us. We will deal with you later," she said.

I turned and started to my room before Daddy said, "No, honey, we are going to deal with this right now."

I had never seen my mama that angry with me, other than that time at church.

Daddy took me by the arm and said, "Sit down here, Samson. You have food all over your shirt. One thing I can say in your defense is that you have always admitted when you were wrong. This is beyond you. It's just not natural for a child your age to eat that much in one sitting. It's just not normal. It's as if you're not yourself."

Then he said with a frown, "Since the time you came home from the hospital, strange things have been happening around here."

I was puzzled and said, "Strange things like what, Daddy?"

He said, "Number one, we had a serious foundation problem on the side of the house where that tree fell. It seemed to have fixed itself. That saved me a lot of money. I'm grateful, but I want to know who fixed it."

He took a few sips of his coffee and said, "I called Joe Hicks about the foundation the other day. I asked him how much I owed him, and he said, 'Nothing.' He said he had not gotten around to us yet."

Daddy looked at me strangely as if he was looking for answers from me. He said, "I'm still trying to figure that one out. Whoever did it, I really want to thank them personally because that's the right thing to do."

He got up from the table and went over to get a slice of cake. He took a bite and said, "As strange as it may seem, I believe you ate all that food. Look at you. I can't understand it. You are almost six feet tall. You look like you've been lifting weights or something. You have muscles everywhere, and you are just seventeen years old. Like I say, I just don't understand what's going on with you. But, what's even stranger is number two. How in the world did you know about the truck on the North Creek side?"

"It was a dream, Daddy. I saw it all in a dream."

He smiled and said, "Well, son, you must be psychic, because your dream became a reality. We went down on the North Creek side, and it was just like you said. There was the truck with a big boulder on it. There were four heads of cattle on the truck that were very weak. There were thirty-five heads of cattle grazing around. A few of them were cut up by some of the sticker bushes. We would have lost them all if it hadn't been for you and your amazing dream. The cuts will heal. I called the sheriff, and he will be here first thing in the morning. You can't see anything out there at night."

I sat there in unbelief as my daddy talked.

"It looked like the truck must have hit the hill where it was parked and shook the boulder loose, causing it to fall on the hood. It was getting dark, but it looked like they even made an access road to get the truck in and out of there without anybody seeing them. We'll know more in the morning. Go on back to bed," he said.

While I was going to my room, Daddy called me back.

"Samson," he said, "if you are going to be eating like this, we won't be able to afford to feed you."

I said, "Yes sir."

Then he said, "And son, I sure was looking forward to one of those turkey legs."

CHAPTER 9

The Sheriff is on the Trail

SEVERAL WEEKS HAD PASSED, AND MAMA WAS still upset with me for eating up everything. I really didn't mean to upset her that way. I believe I was pushing her over the edge.

I heard her and Daddy talking about me in the kitchen. I stood by the door to hear what they were saying. Mama was crying and told Daddy that she was afraid of me. *Afraid of me?* I thought that was very strange. I couldn't believe all that I was hearing.

She said, "Honey, since the day that boy came home from the hospital, he is still acting strange to me. I tell you, I thought it would get better, but it's getting worse. I hear strange noises coming from his room at night. He's talking with someone in his sleep all the time, and he's even sleepwalking."

"Baby, are you sure about all of this? You must remember that he was in a coma. He may still be trying to adjust to being home. No one knows what he was going through while in that coma," Daddy said.

Mom told him she had caught me doing those things several times. She wished she had had a camera so she could show him.

I hadn't realized all of this was going on with me. I really became afraid when she asked Daddy if they needed to let the doctors examine me again. Something hadn't been right with me since the accident. She said it was like I was two different people.

I went back to my room, thinking about what she said. I thought about those strange headaches I had been having. I could never remember going to sleep, just waking up from something like I had been drugged. Who really fixed the house? How did I know about the men and the truck on the North Creek side? Was it a dream, or was it real? Why was I so hungry? Could something really be wrong with me? Maybe I'm going to die. Was that why Mama wanted the doctors to check me out again? Maybe they just didn't want to tell me that. I said to myself, *I'm really going to die.*

I was so afraid. I got down on my knees and prayed. I asked Samson's God to please let me be okay and not let anything be wrong with my brain. I didn't want to die. I prayed until I fell asleep on my knees.

Mama came into my room a little later, woke me up, and told me to get in the bed. She kissed me on the forehead and said, "I love you."

When I woke up, I heard people in the kitchen. I put on my clothes and went in to see who they were. It was a bunch of our neighbors and several officers who came with the sheriff. They were sitting at the table eating. Mama, as usual, had cooked up enough food to feed an army.

I said, "Good morning, Mama and everybody."

Mama smiled and said, "Good morning, Samson. Come on and sit over here and eat your breakfast. Your daddy went with Sheriff Lang down by the North Creek area to check out everything. He said he was so glad you had that dream, because he never would have looked down there in a million years."

Mr. Clark, and some of the neighbors were sitting around the table talking about the North Creek area. He said with a biscuit in his hand, "It turned out those men in the truck had made a road through our properties that went for miles. That road was not far from another road that led to the highway."

Mr. Jameson took a sip of his coffee and said, "Someone had to have surveyed our properties from the sky to do that."

Mr. Chatham said, "Now that's something. That back road gave them access to all our back pastures. That allowed them to take a few of our cattle at a time without us knowing it. Altogether, we have lost nearly a hundred head of cattle in the past six months."

Mama sat a plate in the sink, looked out the door, and said, "Here comes your daddy with the sheriff now."

Daddy came in and washed his hands in the sink. He went over to the stove and got him and the sheriff a few biscuits and bacon. Mama poured them both a hot cup of coffee.

Daddy sat down and said, "You know Samson, I'm so proud of you. You saved all of us thousands of dollars and solved the great mystery of our disappearing cattle. I really feel there's more to this thing than we know."

The sheriff told everybody that he had phoned in the license plates to see who owned the truck and dusted it for fingerprints. "That boulder did a job on that truck," he said.

One of the officers told Daddy he saw a strange set of footprints leading to the house from the North Creek area. "It's kind of strange that they stopped right at your back porch Mr. Avery. Y'all be careful out here," he said.

Daddy looked at me and said, "I want you and your mama to be careful going outside from now on. I'm going to get us a few dogs to help guard the place."

Mr. Morgan took a sip of his coffee, looked over his glasses, and said, "I have a few good dogs I can sell you."

I always wanted a dog, but Daddy hadn't cared that much for them until now.

CHAPTER 10

A New Sheriff in Town

IT HAD BEEN NEARLY SEVEN MONTHS SINCE I WAS last allowed to go away from the house alone. Mama was always afraid that I would do something to hurt myself. She said she didn't want to take any chances on me having a setback.

I decided to take a chance and asked her if I could go down by the creek for just a little while. She thought for a minute and finally said, "It's okay, but please be very careful. The doctors said you are not a hundred percent yet."

I left her to go down by the creek. In my heart, all I wanted was to see my Cynthia, and that would make my day.

I sneaked over, hiding behind the same old bushes as usual. My head started hurting a little, but soon stopped. Immediately, something came over me, and I stood up like a champion. My fears were gone, so I walked over to the crowd. I wasn't afraid anymore. For the first time in my life, I felt I could really take care of myself.

I slowly looked around, and there they were, my worst nightmare: Jason, Eric, and Almond. Looking for their next victim to torture, they were now like three filthy Philistines to me. *Today, things are going to change,* I thought. *There's a new sheriff in town.*

All the kids were so glad to see me and gathered around, asking, "How are you doing, Samson?"

I smiled and said, "I'm doing fine. Just fine."

Little Mickey looked up at me and said, "Wow, Samson! You really got taller."

When he said that, Jason came over with Eric and Almond. All the kids began to move back. They knew there was going to be big trouble.

"Bet you don't got no brains in that big head of yours now since you busted it," said Jason.

I stood there, never saying anything, but I was devising a plan.

Then he started saying, "Samson is so stupid! Samson is so stupid with his no-brain self!"

That's when I started to get angry and said, "Don't call me stupid."

I calmed down and remembered Samson and his riddles. I said, "Jason, what goes out on a limb and comes back wet?"

Everybody started trying to figure out the riddle.

He said, "That don't make no sense. I told you, you were stupid, stupid." He tried to rally the other kids to join him by saying, "Samson is so stupid. Samson is so stupid with that big old knot on his head."

Before I realized it, I pulled back a limb so fast and let it go. It caught Jason right on his butt and flung him into the middle of the creek. No one knew how it happened. It was so funny. Everybody started clapping and laughing at him. However, it was little Rodney Johnson, who Jason had tormented, who got the riddle. He just burst out laughing with all he had. He laughed so hard that everyone else started laughing with him.

He started pointing and laughing, saying, "Jason, it's you. It's you that went out on a limb and came back wet!"

Everyone started pointing and laughing with Rodney, saying, "Look at you now! Look at you now!"

All the other kids at the creek heard us laughing and came over and joined us. They started laughing and pointing at Jason also.

Jason, as wet as a rat, came swimming toward the bank of the creek. He was mad, but I wasn't afraid of him at all. I stood there at the bank of the creek and looked him in the face and said, "Remember, Jason, what goes around comes around."

When I say he was mad, he was mad, but he couldn't say anything as he stood there in the water.

Suddenly, he started jumping and screaming. "Help! Help me, somebody! Please help me! Something is moving in my pants."

A big fish wiggled out of each of his pant legs and onto the ground. That was the funniest thing I had ever seen. He thought they were snakes. Those were nice-size fish too. If he had been in a fishing contest, he probably would have won.

That day, Jason created a brand-new dance, the way he was moving. It was one of the best days I have ever had down at that creek.

Jason was so embarrassed that he ran home crying like little Rodney Johnson, leaving his catch of the day. I didn't think he would cause any more trouble around here again.

Most of the kids were gone, and I went over to pick up the fish, and then it happened. Cynthia came out of nowhere and began talking to me. I couldn't believe it. I didn't go all limp this time. I was very confident in myself. I remembered Samson telling me to stand up like a man if I wanted the women to respect me.

"Samson," she said, smiling, "where did you learn to tell riddles like that?"

I smiled and said, "Oh, it just came into my head."

She said, "That was really neat, but how did you know that was going to happen the way it did?"

I brushed my hair out of my face and simply said, "I don't know."

"Your hair is so long and curly," she said. "Can I touch it?"

Remembering what Samson had taught me, I smiled, bent my head down a little, and said, "Yes, you can touch it."

She took her fingers and pulled them through the locks of my hair and said, "It is longer than I thought. Do you ever cut it?"

I stood up straight and quickly thought about what Samson had also told me about Delilah and said, "No, not lately since I've been sick."

"Samson, I know you've been sick," she said, "but I really miss you in class." She just didn't know. I was ready to tell her all my secrets at that moment. I really had to be strong.

She continued talking. "It hasn't been the same since you've been away. They told us today that we will have the big test next month, so don't forget to study. You won't get promoted if you don't take it. Let me know if you need any help. I will be glad to help you."

I smiled and thanked her, trying to be all macho as she walked away. Standing there like Samson, watching her walk away, I thought, *Now that's some kind of woman.*

Since I had been sick, I had forgotten about the final test. I was glad Cynthia told me about it. You really had to be in a coma or dead to miss that one.

CHAPTER 11

Redemption

EVERYONE WAS FINALLY GONE. I WAS THE ONLY one left at the creek.

As I picked up the fish from Jason's pants, I saw a string coming from the creek. I grabbed the string and pulled it out of the water to find it was full of fish. I couldn't believe it. I picked up all the fish and added Jason's two to the line. I was going to take these babies home to my mama. This would surely make up for me making her so angry when I ate up all the food.

While walking home, I got another bad headache. I sat down by a tree for a while, hoping the headache would pass. I quickly fell asleep and started dreaming. I saw Samson take my fish down by the creek and clean each one of them in a matter of seconds. He sliced and diced them with his knife. He made a fire and cooked four of them for himself and ate them. When he finished eating, he took the rest of the fish and walked away.

I don't know when I got home, but after I did, I found myself in my room studying. I was so glad Cynthia reminded me of the test because I would have been in big trouble had I not remembered it otherwise.

I was just resting in bed and thinking about Cynthia when it happened again! I heard Mama calling me with that voice—that sound that cut right through me. I thought, *Did I eat up all the food again?* I couldn't remember. I was so afraid this time. I had won the battle with Jason, but I was about to lose the war to Mama.

I pulled myself together and went into the kitchen as one to be executed.

"Mama, I'm so sorry," I pleaded.

She said, "Sorry for what? Sugar, did you do this?"

I was shocked and said, "What, Mama?"

"Fish," she said, smiling. "Look at all this fresh fish in the refrigerator, and it's been cleaned. I have never seen so much at one time. Thank you so much, Samson. Your daddy knows I hate cleaning fish."

I stood there just as confused as I could be.

"Samson," she said, "guess what we are having for dinner tonight."

"What, Mama?" I said, puzzled and shaking on the inside.

"Fish! How in the world did you catch so many fish? I didn't even know you could fish."

I was so relieved and said nervously, "It was just my lucky day, Mama. Just my lucky day."

She was so proud of me, saying, "Honey, you have been redeemed! You just keep doing all these amazing things. I just don't know how to take you anymore." She went out of the room, singing, "My baby is a fisherman. My baby is a fisherman." She was so happy.

She quickly stuck her head through the door and said, "Your daddy will be shocked because he can't even fish. My baby is a fisherman."

Having been redeemed, I took a deep breath and slowly walked over to the refrigerator and looked inside. I couldn't believe my eyes. It was loaded with cleaned fish. Trays stacked upon trays of fish! I wondered what was going on.

I went over to the table and sat down, trying to figure this thing out. I felt totally confused. I remembered the two fish from Jason's pant legs, and the fish on the string, but where had all the other fish come from? Then I remembered Samson down by the creek in my dream. Shaking my head, I said, "Oh no! He couldn't have done this. That's impossible. He's just a character in the Bible or is he?" *I must be losing my mind,* I thought.

I started getting a little nervous. I looked in the cabinet and got my medicine. I took it, hoping it would relax my nerves. I prayed with all sincerity and asked God to help me like he helped Samson understand what was going on.

I went back to my room and started hitting the books even though the doctors had not released me to go back to school. They wanted me to take it easy and not strain my brain. For some reason, things had changed tremendously. Reading about Samson had given me a greater desire for reading and a better perception of things. Before, I didn't have that. No matter what the doctors said, I still had to take that test or fail. I was glad Cynthia reminded me.

Mama had forgotten to get the doctor's consent for me to take the test. She told me not to worry and that Daddy would stop by the doctor's office next week while he was in town and get it.

CHAPTER 12

I Can't Believe My Ears

A MONTH OR SO LATER, DADDY HAD TO GO INTO town and pick up some feed for the livestock. I asked if I could go along with him. It was hard being stuck at home on the farm for nearly a year. I wanted to see people. I wanted to see if anything had changed in town.

Daddy took a deep breath and said, "Okay, you can go with me this time."

I was so excited. I hopped in the truck with a big smile on my face. I didn't know how to act.

I didn't have any headaches on the trip. As he drove along the quiet stretch of highway, it was so refreshing. I stuck my head out the window like a dog, letting the wind blow in my face. My hair had really grown. It was blowing all over the place.

Daddy touched me on the shoulder and said, "You know Samson, it's about time for you to get a haircut."

I quickly pulled my head back into the truck and said, "No, Daddy, I'm still having headaches. Don't want any more problems."

I remembered what happened to Samson when they cut his hair off in the story. I quickly pulled my hair back and put it in a ponytail and twisted it.

We finally made it into town, and everything looked so strange to me. Daddy parked the truck, and we both got out. As he headed to Mr. Johnson's feedstore to take care of his business, he said, "Now, don't you wander off too far. Meet me back here at the truck in a couple of hours."

I started walking slowly down the street, checking out the town. It seemed like most of the people didn't recognize me anymore for some odd reason. I recognized all of them. They were looking at me like I was a stranger.

I saw Mr. Dickson, who ran the shoe shop, sweeping his porch while business was slow. He was humming to himself. He would always shine and fix my daddy's shoes. I thought I would stop by and speak to him.

"How are you doing, Mr. Dickson?" I said.

He looked at me, puzzled, and said, "Just fine, son. Now who are you?"

"It's me, Samson, Mr. Dickson. You always shine my daddy's shoes."

"Now, who is your daddy, son?"

"Mr. Avery. I'm Samson Avery, Mr. Dickson."

He took a closer look at me and said, "Samson! Boy, look at you! You done shot up there like one of those tall pine trees. My, look at that ponytail. I didn't realize how long and curly your hair was. You done put on some muscles too. No wonder I didn't recognize you."

He continued looking at me, shaking his head in amazement. He told me that he had heard about my accident and was so glad when people told him that I was okay. He said the whole town had been praying for me. I thanked him for his concern.

He asked, "How is your daddy doing?"

"He's just fine, Mr. Dickson. He went over to the feedstore to get food for the cattle."

"Yes, I heard about them folks stealing your daddy's cows. That's a crying shame. Folks like that need to be strung up like they did back in cowboy days, or horse whipped. I've been keeping my eyes and ears open to see if I hear anything."

I thanked him and told him that I was going over to the ice cream shop. "See you later, Mr. Dickson," I said, walking away.

"All right," he said. "You take care of yourself now." And he went on sweeping his porch.

Just being away from home felt good. Walking over to the ice cream shop, I saw a man who looked kind of familiar to me coming from Mr. Daggard's real-estate office. It was strange because I had never seen him before. *How could I know him? Did I meet him in the hospital while I was in the coma? I may have opened my eyes for a short time or something*, I thought.

Suddenly, I began to follow him against my will. It felt as if someone had taken control of my body, trying to make me follow him. I struggled hard, trying not to follow him, but gave in. I wondered what was going on with me. Was my mind playing tricks on me again?

The man went down the hill to the back of Mr. Hopson's garage. Mr. Hopson always did the work on my daddy's truck. He met another man and gave him some money. I hid behind an old truck parked across the street. I laid there on the ground where I could see them clearly but they couldn't see me.

Then something happened to me that had never happened before. I could hear what they were saying as clear as day from that distance.

I heard the man I followed say to the other man, "They want us to get out of town and cover our tracks fast. They said the sheriff might have a lead on the truck they found smashed on the North Creek side."

The other man said, "How do they know that it was us? There was no evidence."

The other man said, "It don't make no difference. Too much money is at stake for us to mess up this thing now. He gave us fifty thousand dollars apiece to go somewhere and start a new life and never show up around here again. I tell you, I'm out of here."

Suddenly, it hit me. These were the men in my dream who stole our cows. I took the tag numbers of both their vehicles. I was sure the authorities would need this information later. I checked my watch and realized I needed to get back to my daddy's truck. For some strange reason, I had the urge to pick up the truck where I was hiding and smash their cars, but I didn't. I knew I should hurry and take my medicine because I felt strange and light-headed.

I made my way back up the hill to the main road. I could see my daddy loading sacks on the truck. I knew I had to hurry.

As I passed by Mr. Daggard's real-estate office, I noticed the door was partly open. I heard someone talking about the North Creek area. That stopped me in my tracks. *That's our land,* I thought. *What's going on here? This is strange.* Since my accident, it seemed like I have super hearing now.

I heard a man tell another, "They got to have all that North Creek land no matter what. Billions of dollars are at stake, and Mr. Big don't plan to lose one cent of it. You get that land, or you better find me someone who can, if you know what I mean."

I guess the man pulled out a gun and held it to

the other's head because he said, "Please don't shoot." He started crying and said, "Please, I'll get it done. I promise you."

It didn't sound like Mr. Daggard's voice, but the man said, "The last two fools messed things up big time. I'm glad those tags couldn't be traced back to us."

I realized I had stumbled upon the crime of the century, and with mob ties. This was the information my daddy and the sheriff had been looking for. This thing was bigger than all of them. Daddy was right. There was more to it than just stealing cattle. Somebody wanted everybody's land.

My gut feeling told me these men were very dangerous. I couldn't tell my daddy about this now. Someone could get hurt. My daddy could get hurt. It seemed like I had to figure this thing out for myself. I said, "All right, there's a new sheriff in town, and his name is Samson Avery. Get ready for a showdown if that's what you want."

I went on up the street to meet my daddy. He had just finished putting everything on the truck.

"That's good timing, Samson. You get here after I loaded the truck. Did you have a good time?"

"I sure did, Daddy. I sure did." Then I said, "I believe things are about to get pretty exciting around here, like fireworks."

Daddy smiled and said, "You're so right, son. I saw a sign that said the festival starts next week."

Daddy said his goodbyes to everyone at the feedstore, and we headed home. We had gotten a few miles from the house when I noticed a car parked on the side of the road. It looked like one of the cars I had seen at the real-estate office. Daddy thought it was just a broken-down car. Deep down in my gut, I knew there was more to it than what met the eye. I tried to remember the exact spot so I could come back and check it out later.

We knew Mama had cooked another good dinner because the smell met us on the road. Daddy and I tried to figure out what Mama cooked.

Daddy said, "Chicken and dressing, Samson."

I said, "No, steak with rice and gravy."

Then Daddy said, "No, I think it is fried chicken with greens and yams."

I said, "No, Daddy, baked chicken with gravy over rice, green beans, candied yams, and corn bread."

We were having so much fun. The closer we got to the house, the more the smell changed on us.

Daddy finally said, "I smell barbeque." He was so sure of himself that he bet me a dollar that he was right.

He pulled the truck into the shed, and we got out. We went into the house to see what Mama had cooked. We both lost big time and gave her the two dollars. She had a beef roast with potatoes and carrots, turnip greens, stewed apples, corn bread, and pound cake. She had made me some caramel icing on the side to put on my slices.

Daddy smiled and said, "Son, I didn't smell that one coming."

Mama asked us what the money was for, and we told her. She gave me my dollar back and kept Daddy's. She told us to go wash up for dinner.

Mama asked Daddy, "How did things go in town?" and he told her everything went okay and he had gotten a good deal on the feed for the horses.

Then she asked me, "How did things go?"

I said, "It was great getting out of the house. Most of the people didn't recognize me, Mama."

Daddy sat down at the table and told her that they didn't recognized me because I needed a haircut. He laughed and said, "He had his head sticking out the window of the truck, and hair was blowing everywhere. I told him he needed a haircut."

I said, "No, Daddy, I'm not ready for that yet. I don't want any more head troubles right now."

We all laughed and ate our dinner.

CHAPTER 13

Checking Things Out

AFTER DINNER, I WENT TO MY ROOM AND LOOKED out the window, thinking about the car I had seen parked on the side of the road. It really began to torture my curiosity. Something was telling me to go check it out.

I asked Mama and Daddy if it was okay if I went for a walk. Daddy said it was okay and to not let the dark catch me. I took my travel pack with water and my medicine just in case I got a headache.

I had several hours before dark. I started out like I was going down by the creek, where the kids hung out. I knew Mama would be watching me from the window. I headed in the direction of the creek, but when I was out of her sight, I cut through the woods to go up the road to where that car was parked. I found it still there.

There was a big stone near the car. It had been moved and placed there. I could see the marks on the ground where it was moved from. I guess someone put it there to let someone else know where to park. Otherwise, it made no sense to me.

I carefully looked around for footprints and found some. There were several of them. I thought, *Why are these footprints on our property?* I decided to follow them to see where they went.

I got to a point where those footprints led to a man-made path, and I followed it. Someone had smoothed it out, making it passable through all the thick brush. Sitting right smack in the middle of my daddy's land was a trailer, and it wasn't his. How in the world did it get there? No one probably would have ever found it had I not followed that path. My daddy never went down to that part of the North Creek area, and someone knew it, but who?

To my surprise, I saw a group of seven men sitting around talking and drinking beer. I decided to sneak behind the trailer to hear what was going on.

One man said, "The boss wants all this land no matter what. We have less than two months to get the job done. He said this land has everything they need to build his resort."

My ears stood up like a puppy dog's. *A resort,* I said to myself.

Then he said, "They are going to do whatever it takes to get these people off this land and buy it cheap."

Another man said, "They want to spray this land with poison. In two weeks, everything will be dead."

Another man said, "You mean only the grass and crops, right?"

I couldn't believe what I was hearing.

A man in a red-and-black plaid shirt with a hat to match stood up and said, "Everything—birds, animals, and people too if necessary. If it rains, it will get in the soil quicker and destroy everything in a week. If by some chance it gets in the water supply, then people will get sick, and some will eventually die."

A big man smoking a cigar stood up and said, "You mean to tell me they're willing to kill all these folks for this land?"

Things soon started to get scary for all of them when a man in a green plaid shirt stood up, very angry. He pulled out his gun and pointed it at the man, saying, "That means killing you too if it's necessary. Now, what's it going to be?"

The man quickly sat down and said, "Okay, I get it. You don't need the gun. I got it."

The man took a puff from his cigar and began telling them, "Now, the environmental people will come in and test the water and the land and have everybody evacuated until they can find out what's going on.

People will get scared and not want to come back to this place and sell their land dirt cheap. We come in, you see, and buy the land. Then Mr. Big can build his resort with casinos, hotels, restaurants, and shopping malls."

Another man said, "What if someone finds us out here and tells somebody what's going on?"

The other man said, "Look around, you fool! Who do you think is going to come way out here? Nobody! We are too deep in the woods. Let's get ready to go. We'll meet back here in a week around the same time. When the boss gives me the go-ahead, I will let you know."

I hung around until they left. I decided to follow them to see if they were all going the same way. They split up. Three of the men went in one direction, and the other four men went in the direction of the car parked on the side of the road. I decided to follow the three men to see where they were going.

They went about a half mile, and there was a helicopter parked on our property. One of the men said he had to go back to the real-estate office and asked to be dropped off on the east side of the airport to pick up his car.

These people were bold and dangerous. I felt scared for my daddy and all the other people involved with him. These low-down, dirty Philistines wanted to kill everybody, and that made me angry. I had to figure this thing out, and I mean quick. I bet whatever they were going to do, they would use that helicopter to do it with.

I made my way back up to the trailer, and for some strange reason, I wanted to push it over on its side, but I didn't. I hurried back up the path to where that car had been parked, but it was gone. All I could see was the big stone by the road. I moved the stone farther down the road to throw them off their trail the next time. Perhaps this little bit of confusion would slow them down.

It was beginning to get dark, and that spelled trouble for me. My daddy didn't play. I had to rush with all I had. I felt a surge of energy come over me, and I started running. I had never run so fast in my life.

I made it home and wasn't even out of breath. I found Daddy sitting on the porch, waiting on me with his belt in his hands.

"You are one lucky young man, Samson," he said as he put his belt back on. "Get on in here so I can talk to you."

We went in and sat at the kitchen table, and we talked. Daddy told me that the sheriff suspected that there was more to this thing than just the stealing of the cattle.

He said, "They have called in the FBI to help find out what's actually going on. Too many people are involved in this thing."

He said they wanted to thank me again for putting them on the right track. I thought, *If only they knew what I know.*

Daddy went into the sitting room to be with Mama,

and I went to my room. I laid across my bed, thinking about all the stuff that was going on in our little town.

I must have dozed off because I had this strange dream. In the dream, I had all this energy and took off running through the woods, and then I saw Samson hitting something. He was knocking down trees like they were nothing. Trees were falling everywhere, and he was enjoying every minute of it. He was like a boxer throwing punches right and left. He told me he had to let off some steam, and then he walked away.

While he was walking away, he said, "Watch out for those low-down Philistines, Little Sam. Watch out!"

I woke up in the middle of the night hungry as a bear. Whatever was in the refrigerator, I pulled it out to eat. While I was eating, Daddy came into the kitchen.

He said, "Why are you making all that noise and sitting in the dark with the refrigerator open?" Then he turned on the light and said, "Boy, I don't believe this. You are going to eat us out of house and home."

"Daddy," I said, "I'm sorry, but I just couldn't help it. I felt like I was starving."

He told me to finish eating and go back to bed and not get up again. He would have Mama talk to the doctors about my appetite. He pulled something out of my hair and said, "You are definitely getting a haircut if you're going to start growing pine needles in your hair. See you in the morning."

When I woke up, Daddy was out on the front porch talking to some of the neighbors. Apparently, a storm came through during the night and knocked down a whole lot of trees. They had followed the path of the damage and found a trailer on our property. Everybody wanted to know how in the world did it get there. Daddy told me that the sheriff and the FBI were out there investigating. He thought they would probably find a lot of evidence in that trailer.

Then he said, "The funny thing is a storm came through and there was not a drop of rain."

Somebody said, "It had to be mighty strong winds to do something like that."

I asked Daddy if it was okay for me to go look at the damage. He said I could and told me not to get in the way of the sheriff and the FBI.

As I followed the path of the storm, the area looked so familiar to me. That storm made a huge, clean path that allowed me to see for miles. It really looked strange. It had never entered anyone's mind what the land would look like without trees, not to mention the beautiful lakes and streams. Daddy and everybody thanked God for knocking down the trees. It would have cost thousands of dollars to have them cut down. All Daddy had to do now was sell those trees for timber, and the money would come rolling in.

Right smack in the middle of that path of destruction

was the trailer I had seen. I found it amazing how the storm picked that exact area to blow down trees. It was so hard to believe.

The sheriff was collecting cigarette butts, scraps of paper, and whatever else those men left behind for evidence. Suddenly, my head started hurting a little, and I thought about the dream I had where I saw Samson knocking down trees. This path looked like the same area, but that would be impossible. *Samson is a character in the Bible. He's not real,* I told myself.

I couldn't figure out what was going on. I started getting confused again and decided to go back to the house, take my medicine, and get in bed.

It was noontime when I woke up again. Daddy had to meet the sheriff in town with some of the neighbors, and I asked him if I could come along. He smiled and told me to get my things and hop in the truck.

Driving down the road, I could clearly see the place where the storm had blown down all those trees. It was magnificent. I could see why someone would want to build a resort there. That windstorm had revealed some of the hidden treasures of my daddy's land. There was even a beautiful waterfall that I could see in the distance.

Daddy said sadly, "Samson, I never imagined how beautiful this land really was until now. I thank God for that storm."

He had had the wrong idea about the North Creek

area. I thought, *Those men are going to have to find themselves another meeting place now, for sure.*

I unbraided my ponytail and stuck my head out the window. The wind felt so good blowing in my face while my hair blew all over the place.

Daddy touched my shoulder and told me to put my head back in the truck. He said, "If you keep that up, I'm going to get you a haircut, for sure. I have never seen anyone's hair grow as fast as yours."

We finally made it into town, and Daddy went over to the sheriff's office with the other neighbors. He asked me to meet him back at the truck in a couple of hours. I asked him for some money. I wanted to stop by Mike's Grill and get something to eat. He gave me $15 and told me not to spend it all in one place.

I was so hungry. I went on over to Mike's Grill and placed my order. Believe it or not, I ordered four large cheeseburgers with the works, three large orders of fries, three large sodas, and a big slice of cake with two scoops of ice cream on top. My total came to $13.87.

I took a seat near the window. From there, I could look out and see everything while I waited for my food. I could see my daddy and the neighbors talking with the sheriff. Other people started to join them. I sat there, looking from building to building, hoping to see anything suspicious. I saw nothing, but I was beginning to feel strange.

The waitress brought my order and asked, "Are you going to eat all this food by yourself, or is someone coming to join you?"

"I'm eating it all myself," I said, smiling.

"Are you sure? I just don't believe you can eat it all by yourself," she said, looking at me puzzled.

Knowing my mischievous nature, I smiled and said, "What would you like to bet?"

"What about another scoop of ice cream if you finish half of it?" she said.

My confidence level had risen one hundred percent. I said, "I tell you what; if I eat everything on my plate, I want a refill of everything."

She was so sure I couldn't do it. She looked around at her boss, who nodded to give her the go-ahead.

She smiled and said, "Okay, but if you lose, you have to do the dishes."

I looked at her and said, "That's fine with me." She just didn't know how great that made me feel.

She was so confident that I couldn't eat all my food. She told some of the people in the restaurant that I was going to eat everything I ordered in one sitting. They all came over and looked at my food on the table and put up their bets. The excitement was on. They, like her, believed I couldn't eat it all. There was $70 at stake. I only had $15, plus I had to pay for my food out of that.

I didn't have to pray this time. I was just that hungry.

I sat there and ate one huge burger after another like it was nothing and ate all my fries.

Someone said, "This kid can't be real."

I drank my large sodas and ate my cake with ice cream on top until all of it was gone. Then I gave a loud belch of satisfaction.

"Excuse me," I said.

The waitress was shocked, as was everyone else. Unfortunately for them, I was still hungry. No one could believe I ate all that food.

Disappointed that she lost the bet, she tried to compose herself and said, "Do you want your refill to go?"

I smiled and said, "No. I'll eat it right here."

She bucked her eyes and said, "Everything, again?"

Things really began to heat up then. Everyone placed another bet that I couldn't eat the same amount of food again. To their surprise, I ate everything, asked for a glass of water, and gave out an even louder belch. No one could believe it.

My lunch had brought me an easy $200. I was feeling full and fine. I took my money off the table and put it in my pocket. I got up, thanked everyone, and left with the waitress looking confused and shaking her head.

CHAPTER 14

Someone is Following Me

HAVING EATEN A MOST FILLING LUNCH AND HAVING $200 in my pocket, I decided to walk around town and do a little investigating of my own. I felt like I could fly. I had so much energy. Suddenly, my body started swelling, but I felt fine this time.

I walked on down the hill to where I had seen the two men the last time I came to town with Daddy. Something strange caught my attention. There was a large mirror sitting next to the wall outside the furniture repair shop. As I passed by, looking at the mirror, I thought I saw someone following me. I looked around and didn't see anyone. Whoever he was, he certainly had a lot of hair on his head and muscles.

I decided to look around to see where he went. It was the strangest thing. There was nowhere he could go without being seen, but this fellow had disappeared on me.

There was a hill not too far away. I decided to go up to the top of it. Perhaps I could spot the person who had been following me. I was also curious to see what was on the other side of the hill.

I took off running up the hill and didn't break a sweat. I reached the top in no time. I looked to see if I could see that person who had been following me. He was nowhere to be seen. I looked toward the woods and saw two trucks and a car traveling a winding dirt road. I found that odd when most of the people wanted to know what was going on back at the sheriff's office.

I had about an hour before I had to meet Daddy back at the truck. Something forced me to follow that road. Instinctively, I just took off running through the woods, jumping over little streams, and going up and down hills, and it felt great.

I made it to a clearing, and I saw another trailer like the one found on my daddy's land. I couldn't believe it. I decided to wait for the trucks to arrive and see what was going on. I had a funny feeling these people were hiding from someone.

They pulled up to the trailer and got out of their vehicles, just fussing at each other. One said, "I can't believe that a storm hit in the exact spot where our trailer was and didn't hit the trailer. What are the odds of something like that happening?"

Another one said, "Yeah, what are the odds of a boulder smashing our truck? I tell you, something strange is going on out there at the North Creek. I'm beginning to get a bad feeling about this deal."

Another one said, "If anything else happens, I am out of here for sure."

They all went into the trailer, sat down, and poured themselves a drink and continued to talk. I peeped through the window. They were really scared and felt the sheriff was going to find out something sooner or later. They drank until they all fell asleep.

I felt like doing something mischievous. I couldn't help myself. I had to do something. I took a tire off each of their vehicles and threw them far into the woods. Then I turned over their trailer, with the door to the ground. Those men were still in the trailer. That really woke them up! They were scared out of their senses and screaming for their lives. I took off running as happy as I could be to meet my daddy. All I could here was the men saying, "Help! Somebody please, help us!" "Don't tell me it's another storm!" "Help! Somebody help us!"

They had forgotten that they were calling for help way out in the middle of nowhere. No one would hear them. They were going to have to figure out how to get out of that trailer and out of those woods before dark.

I made my way down the hill and past that mirror and saw that same person following me again. I turned around, and he was gone. I couldn't understand it.

I had only ten minutes to make it back to Daddy's truck. This time, I was all out of breath when I got there.

Daddy was sitting in the truck, waiting for me. He said, "Boy, you had me worried. Are you okay? Why are you breathing so hard?"

"Oh, I ran so I wouldn't be late, Daddy," I said.

He smiled and said, "Get on in this truck."

I must have fallen asleep because the next thing I knew, Daddy was waking me up. He pulled into the shed, and we got out.

He said, "Samson, are you okay? You fell asleep when you got in the truck."

I knew he was worried about me. I smiled and said, "I'm just fine, Daddy. I really got a lot of exercise today."

We went into the house and found Mama had fixed another great dinner. We washed up and got ready to eat. While sitting at the table, Mama asked Daddy what happened in town. I was eager to know what happened.

He took a swallow of iced tea and said, "The FBI believe that somebody wants everybody's land. They started stealing most of our cattle first to create fear and confusion, thinking people would be so concerned about the lost cattle and wouldn't be expecting anything else. They are probably going to try to scare us off our land eventually. The sheriff said this is what happens when the mob gets involved."

I said, "The mob? What's the mob doing here in Soyerville, Daddy? This is really bad news."

He said, "Well do I know, son. The FBI did a survey of everybody's property from the air. It's all marked off with red, yellow, and blue markers as far as you can see. There was even a place to land a helicopter. No one knows how or when they did all of this. The sheriff said they had the photos analyzed, and it looks like someone wants to put up some sort of resort on our properties, and it's huge. I can't believe this. Somebody is just going to take my land without even making me an offer."

I sat there quietly thinking about everything Daddy said. Those men were scared because someone had put the pressure on them. Now I know the reason why.

That Mr. Big must be the mob boss. If that's the case, I don't think he's going to give up on his plan without a fight. These uncircumcised Philistines are probably going to do something drastic, and I'm going to be ready for them, I said to myself.

CHAPTER 15

The Philistines are Back

A FEW WEEKS LATER, I GOT UP EARLY AND WENT into the kitchen. Mama already had my breakfast on the table. I was so hungry and ate as fast as I could. Anxious, I couldn't sit still. I had something on my mind. I just had to go down and investigate the area that was in those photos. Daddy and some of the neighbors were already up and about.

Mama said, "Honey, I haven't seen you reading your Bible lately. Have you lost interest in Samson already?"

I smiled and said, "No way, Mama. Samson is my inspiration. He's my hero. He has changed my life."

She smiled and said, "That's really good."

I asked her if I could go down by the North Creek area and look around with Daddy and the others. She said I could and to be very careful. She felt more comfortable about me going down there since the storm had cleared the area. Trucks had come in and hauled away most of the fallen trees.

I packed a lunch with water, juice, and my medicine just in case my head started hurting, and headed for the North Creek area. I went looking for what everyone else may have missed in the investigation. One thing was, of all the places they could have placed that trailer in the photo, why that spot? It was as if they were hiding or guarding something there.

I decided to go down to where the trailer may have been. I climbed a tree near that trailer. I went up as high as I could to look around. Suddenly, my head started hurting again. I started climbing down to be safe. But a surge of energy came over me, and I climbed to the very top of that tree. I could see for miles. I saw some of the red, yellow, and blue markers, and an area marked off by chains. That trailer was positioned several yards in front of those chains. The red areas were by the lake. The blue areas were by the hills. The yellow areas were in the clearing, but the chains—what were they for? I guessed the FBI couldn't see them from the air.

Now I was curious as to what those chains were for, and how far they went into the woods. I thought, *How can someone come in and take over folks' land without their permission like that?* I was getting angrier by the minute. These people were very bold and very dangerous.

I climbed down the tree to head to the area where I saw the chains. When I reached the ground, Samson was there waiting for me.

"How are you doing there, Little Sam?" he asked.

I frowned and said, "Kind of angry right now."

"Ah," he said, "now you see what I was telling you about those low-down, dirty Philistines?"

"Yeah, but I didn't think people like that lived right here in Soyerville."

He looked at me, shook his head, and smiled as we walked on down to the area where the chains were.

He began to tell me the story of the Philistines and how bold they were. He said, "Those Philistines made my people's lives miserable. They tormented them day in and day out for forty years." He sighed and said, "Once a Philistine, always a Philistine, Little Sam. It doesn't matter how much you love them. They will always sell you out. They put so much fear into my women that they even betrayed me. I believe these people you are dealing with will do the same thing to your family unless we can stop them."

We walked deep into the woods following the chains. Suddenly, we noticed something strange. There was this sticky, black stuff coming up out of the ground. A pool of it was just bubbling up.

Then I suddenly realized what it was. I yelled, "This is oil! My daddy is rich! Samson, it's oil! My daddy is rich!"

He looked at it, smelled it, and said, "I hope your daddy is rich, Little Sam. This is oil, all right. This is the main reason why someone wants this land. Those markers may be for a resort, true enough, but these people want this oil and will do anything to get it."

I thought about the man who said billions were at stake and Mr. Big didn't want to lose one penny of it. Now I see what he was talking about.

Samson said, "Little Sam, now let's hurry and get a sample and tell your daddy so he can get someone out here to check it out. Those low-down, dirty Philistines may have already filed a false claim on this land just to get the rights to the oil."

I looked in my bag and took out a small jar to put the oil in. When I looked up, Samson was gone.

I made my way back up to the trailer and decided to take a rest behind it. I had started eating my lunch when I heard voices coming from the trailer. I couldn't believe the nerve of these people. I took my medicine just in case there was trouble. I slowly peeped in the window, and there were three men talking this time.

One man said, "Mr. Big wants these people off this land now! He doesn't care if we torch the place. All this land is worth billions to him. If we can't get the job done, he said we will never see the sun shine again."

Another man said, "What's the big deal, anyway? He

can afford to build a resort anywhere. Why here? Why this place? It's like it's haunted or something."

Another said, "Did you hear what he said? They are going to kill us if we can't get this land."

Unexpectedly, a lizard crawled up my pant leg, and I hollered. I was trying to get it out. The men came rushing out of the trailer. I took off running with the lizard still in my pants. I was running and trying to beat that lizard out of my pants at the same time. They took off running after me. I was running for dear life.

One man must have pulled out his gun, because I heard someone say, "Don't shoot the kid!"

For some strange reason, I decided to let them catch me to get more information. I didn't know if I was doing the right thing, but I did it anyway. I threw my backpack as far as I could up the path in case Daddy walked that way looking for me. I had marked the container with the oil in it with the location where I found it. I had placed it in my backpack with my medicine. This would give Daddy a head start in getting the legal rights on the oil if I wasn't found.

While running, I pretended to trip and fall, and they finally caught me. I struggled with them to get free. They tied my arms behind me and took me back to the trailer and sat me in a chair. Then they began asking questions.

"What are you doing around here, boy?"

"Where do you live?"

"What did you hear?"

Looking from one to the other, I said, "This is my daddy's land you're on. I always walk around here. You said somebody was going to kill you about something. That's all I heard."

Things started turning bad for me. I was a witness, and I had heard too much, plus I could recognize each of them.

One of the men said, "We've got to get rid of him, kid or no kid. He knows too much. We are already in enough trouble and don't need any more. There's a well not too far from here. We'll throw him in there. No one will ever find this nosy, little runt."

I thought, *Oh my goodness, what have I gotten myself into? I should have kept running while I had the chance.*

They tied me up even tighter, took me out, and threw me in the trunk of their car. They slowly drove down the path near the well.

The car suddenly stopped, and they opened the trunk. Two of the men grabbed me by both arms and legs like I was a sack of potatoes. They carried me until they came to the well and finally sat me down. Tired and frustrated, they decided to take a rest.

The rag came off my mouth, and I yelled as loudly as I could, "Samson! Samson please help me!" He never showed.

One of the men said, "Ain't no Samson around here, boy. It's just you and us. Now shut up!"

They covered my mouth again and sat down.

While waiting there like an animal getting ready for the slaughter, I remembered how Samson prayed. He told me how he prayed to his God when he was in trouble, and his God heard him. I was in trouble now. I prayed that his God would hear me.

The men got up, grabbed me, and started to throw me in the well when one of them said, "Do we really have to kill the kid?"

Another one said, "It's either him or you. Which do you prefer?"

They decided to throw me in the well. I braced myself for the impact. Samson had taught me pretty much everything I needed to survive. He taught me how to fall into and get out of a well. This time was different. My hands weren't tied then, and there wasn't any oil involved.

Before I hit the bottom of the well, I got a very bad headache. Unexpectedly, all the ropes they had tied me with broke just like that. I floated up to the top to get a breath of air when I heard their car drive away.

Ironically, I began to swell up again, and my sixth sense kicked in. I braced myself against the wall of the well and tried to make my way up. I was so glad I grew those extra inches. It took me awhile to get out because the well was so slippery from the oil. Samson's God had heard my prayers and helped me get out of that well. I gladly thanked him.

I found myself covered in thick, black oil that was in this second well. This was probably how they discovered all the oil on our property when they drew water from the wells to drink. I was convinced somebody found this oil while hunting on our land. *Who was it?* I wondered.

I made my way up to that trailer as fast as I could. I had the urge to climb a tree to see how far those men who threw me into the well had gone. They were not that far ahead of me. They probably thought I was dead and they had no need to rush.

I ran and caught up with them without them knowing it. Suddenly, I started swelling all over, again. I had so much energy. I started kicking several trees, and they fell on their car, trapping the men inside. I leaned against a tree, and it fell on the car too. Those men were going to remain there for a long while.

I hurried on home to tell Daddy what happened, picking up my backpack along the way.

CHAPTER 16

Not Dead Yet

AFTER NEARLY AN HOUR AND A HALF, I FINALLY made it out of those woods. Totally drained of energy, I fuzzily saw my daddy in the backyard in the distance. Relieved, I called to him as loudly as I could. "Daddy! Daddy help me!"

He looked in my direction, dropped what was in his hands, and came running to me as fast as he could. All my energy was just about gone as I staggered across the yard.

Daddy had never seen me in a condition like this. He took one look at me, took a deep breath, and said frantically, "Oh my goodness! Son, are you okay? What happened to you?"

As I fell on his shoulders, he tried with all he had to hold me up. "Samson, what did you do this time?"

"Daddy," I said, "nothing! Please, let me explain. Don't get upset. I need to catch my breath."

I was so exhausted at the time. He helped me across the yard where I could sit down.

I told him everything. Even in my weakness, I was so excited. "Daddy, there's oil on our land, and somebody wants it bad!"

Daddy looked at me as he sat me on the bench and said, "What do you mean, oil? Ain't no oil around these parts, son."

I said, "Look at me, Daddy. Just look at me! I'm covered in oil. Smell me!"

He leaned over and smelled me. I saw the confusion in his face. I had never seen my daddy like this before.

I said, "Daddy, you are a very rich man. I found three men in another trailer farther down by the North Creek area. They were told to do whatever it took to get our land. I was hiding outside the trailer when I heard them. A lizard ran up my pant leg, and I hollered. That's the only reason why they caught me. They tied me up, put me in the trunk of their car, drove down to another well, and threw me in."

Daddy couldn't believe all I was saying. He shook his head and said, "They did what?"

"Daddy, that's how I got all this oil all over me," I said. "I tried as hard as I could to crawl out of the well, and I did. They were trying to get out of those woods so fast. I heard a loud noise, and they may have run into a tree or something, because I heard something fall."

My daddy was spellbound as I told him what had happened to me. He called Mama and told her to get me some clean clothes. He insisted that we were going to the sheriff's office. I told him that I had taken a sample of the oil from a puddle that had chains around it and that it was in my backpack.

I asked seriously, "Daddy, is this oil stuff going to come out of my hair?"

He looked at my head and managed to smile, saying, "Samson, this oil is so thick in your hair they just might have to cut it all off to get it out."

I really wanted to die when he said that.

Mama wrapped me in a blanket to keep me warm and protect the truck from the oil. We hopped in the truck and headed to the sheriff's office. I was slimy wet and sliding in my clothes in the seat as Daddy quickly drove us into town.

He looked over at me and said, "That's a powerful smell you got on you. Stay in the truck until I can make sure no one is smoking around the building or in the office when we get out. Don't want you going up in flames."

I was quite sure nothing would happen, but like my daddy, I didn't want to take any chances. I was going to sit until he gave me the okay.

Daddy pulled up to the sheriff's office, looked around, peeped in, and told me, "Come on."

He went in yelling like a crazy man. "Sheriff! Hey, Sheriff, they tried to kill my boy! Sheriff, where are you? They tried to kill my boy!"

The sheriff came running out of his office, saying, "What's wrong, Mr. Avery?"

Daddy took a deep breath and said, "Sheriff, those people that want our land tried to kill Samson. They were out there today in another trailer. There is oil on my land, Sheriff! Look at Samson! He's covered in it. They threw him in a well, but he got out. He said the men are still out there trapped in a car."

The sheriff looked at my daddy like he was shocked at what he was saying. He took a deep breath and scratched his head for a few moments.

"Have a seat, Mr. Avery," he said, helping Daddy into the chair. "Somebody bring him a glass of water over here. Calm down, Mr. Avery, and let me get this straight. Samson is covered in all that black oil because somebody threw him into a well on your property?"

"That's right, Sheriff. They threw my boy into a well. He could have been killed!"

"I know something major is going on out there, but I didn't think it would come to something like this. We'll take pictures of Samson since he's wearing the evidence and ask him a few questions," said the sheriff.

I was standing there in a puddle of oily gunk that had drained from my clothing when the sheriff said, "Stand over there by the yellow footprints, Samson. Jim is going to take some pictures of you."

They took pictures of me and took evidence off my clothes and my hair, putting it in tiny cups. The sheriff told me to go to the back and take a shower and then come back and talk to him.

It took me the longest time to get that thick oil out of my hair. There were several bottles of shampoo and conditioners back there, and I used all of them. I was so glad it now seemed I didn't have to get a haircut.

When I opened the shower door, all the steam from the shower filled the room, and I could hardly see. After that, I quickly put on my clothes and went out to talk with the sheriff. I told him everything my daddy had told him.

The sheriff quickly called the FBI, and they arrived at the office in less than an hour.

The FBI asked, "Can you show us the area where that car is, Samson? How many people were in the car?"

I said, "Yes, sir, I can show you. There were three of them in the car."

They continued to ask me questions. I told them the same things that I had told my daddy.

The sheriff got excited and yelled, "Everybody, let's get ready to hit the trail!"

All of them quickly jumped into their vehicles and cranked up to go deep down to the North Creek area.

Before we drove off, I quickly hopped out of Daddy's truck and said, "Wait a minute, Sheriff! I forgot to tell you that everybody is going to need lots of water and a lunch. It's going to take us a long time to get there."

He said, "How long do you think it's going to take?"

I said, "Oh, about two or three hours, depending."

The sheriff cleared his throat and said, "Two or three hours depending on what?"

"The condition of your men, Sheriff. If we must stop walking and rest a lot, that's going to take us longer."

The sheriff said, "Oh, I see. Hold up, everybody," he yelled. "You all need to go pack yourselves a good lunch for this trip. According to Samson, it's a two- or three-hour journey down into those woods. Get lots of water, a backpack, and probably some oxygen." He turned, looked at me, and said, "Samson said you're really going to need it."

We were like a convoy driving down the road. When we arrived at our place, we drove down to the North Creek area as far as we could go in our vehicles.

The sheriff got out and began to stretch before the walk. He looked around and said, "Mr. Avery, this sure is a beautiful piece of land. That windstorm really did this place a favor."

Daddy said, "It sure did, Sheriff. It sure did."

The sheriff took a deep breath and yelled, "Okay, everybody, let's hit the trail." Then he turned to me and said, "Lead the way, Samson."

We all walked way down past the trailer, and way down another path. They all thought I was kidding.

We had been walking for nearly an hour, and most of them were already out of breath, sweating and needing to take a water break. After the break, we hit the trail again.

It took us nearly another hour to reach the car's location. They saw all the trees that had fallen on the car and wondered what had happened.

The sheriff looked at Daddy and said, "Mr. Avery, you sure have a lot of trees falling on your property. This car didn't hit the tree. These trees, for some strange reason, hit this car. How in the world could that have happened? This is a very mysterious situation here, Mr. Avery."

The three men were still there inside the car. Several of the men with us had to cut some limbs away from the car to get to the men inside. To our surprise, they all appeared to be dead. They had shot themselves, and blood was everywhere. The sheriff was shocked. He didn't expect any deaths. Unfortunately, someone had to go all the way back to his car and call for the coroner to meet us. Even though we were all hungry, no one could eat after seeing such a gruesome crime scene.

The coroner arrived with paramedics after a few hours. They pulled the men out of the car. Two of them were, in fact, dead, but one still had a pulse and was hanging on by a thread. He was quickly taken to the hospital. The sheriff hoped he would live long enough for him to get some information from him later.

These men were so terrified of that Mr. Big, whoever he is, that they were willing to kill themselves. He has to be somebody here in Soyerville, I thought. Who in town had that kind of power?

After the coroner and sheriff finished with the dead, Daddy asked me to show them where the well and the oil were. We headed for the well and did an awful lot of walking again. They were huffing and puffing like crazy.

The sheriff, wet with sweat and huffing, told me to slow down so they could all catch their breath. He said, "Samson, it's been a long time since I had this much exercise."

We rested awhile, ate our lunch, and then got back on the trail.

We finally made it to the spot, and I showed them where the well was. The evidence was still there. We could see where I had crawled out of the well with oil on me. The oil was all over the well and in my footprints on the ground. One of the deputies took pictures while the FBI collected evidence. After that, everyone took a deep breath, and we headed down behind the trailer.

While we were walking, the sheriff asked, "How in the world did you get out of that well, Samson? It looked like it was really deep."

I said, "It was real deep, Sheriff." I couldn't tell him the truth. I said, "I really don't know how I did it. Maybe it was my adrenaline. They say it can make you strong at times. I guess I was so scared that it gave me strength to get out. All I remember is fighting for my life to get out of that well, and I did."

He said, "Samson, you're one extraordinary young man."

I pointed and said, "There's the oil over there, just bubbling. See?"

Daddy and the sheriff went over to the bubbling pool and looked at it. My daddy put his hands on his head, turned around, and then took a deep breath. He couldn't believe his eyes, and neither could the sheriff. They were both speechless, and so was everyone else. None of us had ever seen oil like this. One of the FBI men took pictures of everything.

The sheriff said to my daddy, "Mr. Avery, it looks like you are going to be a mighty rich man around these parts. You own most of the land around here."

My daddy just stood there, numb. It was hard for him to comprehend everything. He couldn't seem to believe the magnitude of this thing. He was going to be super rich!

Everyone geared up for the long walk home. They were totally exhausted. The sheriff asked my daddy if he knew how much land he owned and how far it went. My daddy was still in shock. He just shook his head and didn't say anything as we headed back to the house.

I said, "Daddy, it looked like those men marked our land off really good!"

CHAPTER 17

Hungry as a Bear

MAMA DIDN'T COME WITH US WHEN WE WENT DOWN on the North Creek side to see the oil. She stayed behind to fix dinner for everyone. Whatever it was she was cooking, it made its way through those woods, attacked our noses, and held us hostage. The smell hit all of us at the same time out of the clear blue. Our stomachs were rumbling and growling like bears. We had all worked up a mighty appetite. To be honest, I could have eaten a whole roasted grizzly.

We were so excited when we saw the house in the distance. Everybody was puffing and saying, "Hallelujah!" We reached the backyard, all drenched in sweat. We all stopped and took a deep breath before going on the porch. Daddy knocked on the back door as we brushed ourselves off.

Mama opened the door with a big smile on her face. She asked everyone to come on in and get some water. She had glasses of cold water ready for us.

"I saw y'all coming across the yard when I peeped out the window. Go on in and wash up. I have food on the table for you," she said, smiling.

We all went into the house, washed up, and took our seats at the table. We couldn't wait to fix our plates. All the hands went to the mountain of fried chicken at the same time. We were so hungry. We passed the ham, dressing, green beans, cabbage, sweet potatoes, squash, gravy, and rolls. We all poured ourselves a big glass of iced tea to wash it all down. Suddenly, there was pure silence. No one spoke a word. We just ate, and ate, and ate.

Finally, there was dessert. Mama had made a huge old-fashioned peach cobbler in a great big iron pot. Daddy had to help her bring it to the table. It was simply delicious, and we all went for seconds and thirds.

When we couldn't eat any more, Mama fixed plates for some of them to take home. We all got up, patted our stomachs, and sat on the front porch to relax. The next thing I knew, everyone was asleep, including the FBI.

Mama smiled and said, "Just let them sleep, sugar. I can see they are tired. Knowing you like I do, you probably walked them nearly to death."

When they finally woke up, they all thanked Mama for the delicious dinner and went on their way.

The sheriff said, "Mr. and Mrs. Avery, thank you again for the delicious meal and my plate. I'm going over to the hospital to check on that man. I hope he's able to give us some information. Mr. Avery, I need you and Samson to stop by my office tomorrow to meet with the FBI again."

Daddy was so exhausted. He sat down in his chair and went to sleep again. I was so excited and told Mama that the sheriff had told Daddy he was going to be a mighty rich man, finding oil on our property.

She dropped down in her chair and said, "Oh my Lord. They found oil on our property, here in Soyerville?"

Excitedly, I said, "Yes, Mama, and I mean lots of it. It was bubbling all out of the ground."

Mama sat there in her rocker, speechless for a while. I decided to leave her alone. I knew the next thing she would do was go into her quiet room and talk to the Lord about it.

There are a lot of oil wells in Texas, but I never thought we would one day have one of our very own. I laid across my bed, looking up at the ceiling trying to imagine just how rich we were really going to be. The ceiling was suddenly covered with nothing but dollar signs and hearts. *Daddy just might get me a real truck now,* I thought. *Look out Cynthia. Here I come!*

Daddy finally woke up, went into the kitchen, and got another big bowl of peach cobbler. He was excited to tell Mama the good news. Before he could say anything, she told him what I had told her about the oil.

I heard him say, smiling, "That boy is just like an old refrigerator. He just won't keep nothing."

He called me with a very peaceful voice. I knew I wasn't in any trouble this time. I went in and sat down to see what he wanted.

He looked at me with tears in his eyes and said, "Thank you, son. If it wasn't for you, this blessing would have never come our way."

CHAPTER 18

It Fell from the Sky

A FEW DAYS HAD GONE BY, AND I WAS ANNOYED. IN my mind, I felt like finding the oil wasn't a blessing for us just yet. I could really feel more trouble brewing. This thing wasn't over. Someone had gone through a lot of trouble trying to get everyone's land. I knew that person was still out there.

I asked Mama if it was okay for me to go down by the creek with the kids for a while before it got too late, and she said I could go. I had to do some more investigating.

Daddy said, "Samson, I want you to go into town with me tomorrow so we can record our find and make some contacts, okay?"

I smiled and said, "Yes sir."

In my mind, I could hear Samson saying, "Keep your eyes and ears open, Little Sam."

Anxiously, I grabbed my backpack with a snack, some water, and my medicine and started toward the creek. When I was out of my mama's sight, I headed down to the North Creek area again. I had this burning feeling that I would find something more down there.

Suddenly, Samson appeared out of nowhere.

He said, "Hurry and follow me, Little Sam."

I knew whenever Samson appeared like this, there would be big trouble. The blood of those Philistines was in the air, and I could smell it.

We went down the back side of the North Creek and heard voices. My instincts were right. We hid behind the large boulders to see what was going on. There were a lot of men down there, removing all the evidence from the scene. *Someone must have tipped them off,* I thought. Little did they know the FBI had all the evidence they needed to crack the case. *That Mr. Big and his gang must be really scared.* Amazingly, there was a helicopter lifting the trailer off the ground to relocate it.

I thought I recognized a few of the men. From a distance, one looked like the mayor, but I couldn't be sure, with all the dust that was flying. Could this be Mr. Big? I couldn't believe the mayor of our city would stoop so low if it was him.

Samson became so angry that sweat was popping off him. He pulled up a tree from the ground and threw it at those men.

"Don't just stand there, Little Sam. Do something! Let's get these low-down, dirty Philistines," he yelled.

I picked up a giant boulder and threw it at the helicopter. No one knew what was going on. They were all caught off guard. That trailer fell to the ground and smashed into a million pieces. The helicopter started flying out of control and tumbled down behind it. I had smashed its propeller. All the men were hurt in some way and were running and yelling for their lives.

"What's going on out here? I told y'all this place was haunted. Wait for me," one of them said.

Another said, "We're under attack! Run!"

They ran as fast as they could to get out of there. A couple of them had gotten trapped by some of the debris. The man who looked like the mayor was hurt badly. Blood was running from everywhere on him. Several of the men had to help carry him. He seemed scared to death, telling the men, "Hurry up and get me out of here, please."

The helicopter crash caused a fire that could be seen for miles, but it soon burned out.

Later, the sheriff and the FBI were back on our property, trying to figure out what in the world was going on. Someone had reported the fire.

The sheriff scratched his head and said, "I just can't understand it, Mr. Avery. Why does it seem like all these strange things only happen on your property? It's like a guardian angel is watching over you or something."

The sheriff continued looking around with the FBI. He pointed and said, "Look over there. More big trees have been uprooted. Please, don't nobody tell me we had another storm."

I left from watching the sheriff in the distance and went looking for Mr. Big and his gang. They had no transportation, so I knew it was going to take them a long while to get to their vehicles.

I climbed up a tree to see where they were. I spotted them. They looked like a bunch of wounded Philistines who had lost the battle, sitting under a tree. Ahead of them, I saw some of the others struggling to make their way to the main road. Some were falling and losing blood.

I must say, this was an exciting evening for me and Samson. I went on back to the house, and Samson went on his way. Daddy had no idea that I was at the North Creek area.

I was home when Daddy made it back all out of breath. I had forgotten to check my hair. He took one look at me and said, "Samson, what's all that stuff in your hair? Didn't I tell you that if it happened again, you would get it cut off?"

I said, "Yes sir," and begged him to not cut my hair.

He told me to take a bath and get ready for bed. We had to get up early in the morning.

CHAPTER 19

Planning My Strategy

I COULDN'T WAIT FOR MORNING TO COME SO I COULD go into town with my daddy. I still had to do a little more investigating on my own. I wanted to go by the mayor's favorite hangout, the donut shop. If he wasn't there, I knew he would probably be somewhere around town hiding or up to no good. Since so many people had been injured, I wanted to see just how many men would be wearing bandages or limping around town.

I decided to read some more about Samson before I finally went to sleep. I knew the story by heart because I had memorized it. What was so exciting was that every time I read the story, I gained a new experience or a new discovery about Samson, as well as about myself.

I soon found myself sitting by the creek with him not far from one of the Philistine villages. He was cooking fish over the fire. It smelled so good. I noticed he appeared sad.

I said, "What's wrong, Samson?"

He removed some of the wood from the fire and asked me to run with him. We took off running along the shore, climbing hills and jumping over cliffs.

Every time I would ask him a question, he would say, "Keep up, Little Sam."

Finally, he got to a point and took a deep breath. He looked over toward a village not that far away.

He said, "Take a good look at that village down there, Little Sam. It looks normal, but it's not. There's danger everywhere. Sometimes, you must trust your gut and keep your eyes and ears open. Trust no one, no matter how well you think you know them. Be cautious and be very careful. Many times, it will be those people that will betray you or even kill you. Keep your eyes and ears open tomorrow and remember all the things I taught you. Your life and your parents' lives are depending on it. You have already seen what those Philistines can do, and they know who you are. Tomorrow, Little Sam, they will not recognize you."

As we walked back to camp, he sadly pointed to the sun and said, "Look at the sky, Little Sam. You see, the sun is going down. Remember, everything has an end."

I didn't understand the story about the sun, but I hoped he would explain it to me later. We reached camp and sat down. He took a nice-size fish to eat and gave me one. We ate all we could, and then he thought for a few minutes.

He said sadly, "Little Sam, I will be leaving you soon, and I will see you no more. I want you to know I thank you for allowing me to be part of your world."

I couldn't believe he was leaving me. I broke down and began to cry. "No! Please don't leave me now! I need you, Samson. You are my best friend. Please don't leave me!"

Tears ran down my face. I had no one else in my life like him or that I wanted to be like. He shook me and told me to control myself.

He said, "Things like this don't happen, Little Sam. I have lived my life. Apparently, God had a special purpose for you, and he needed my help. I guess my purpose was to teach you about life and prepare you for the journey ahead. Your daddy really needed you at this time in his life. Otherwise, those uncircumcised Philistines would have stolen everyone's land and his oil."

I tried to hold back the tears and act like the man he had taught me to be, and said, "I know, Samson, but it still hurts to see you go."

He said, "Look at me, Little Sam, and don't you ever forget what I'm about to tell you. You are an incredible young man. In fact, you are no ordinary superhero. You are an extraordinary one. You will continue to be the 'Samson' of your times, as I was in mine."

I thought that was something coming from Samson. I wiped the tears from my eyes, smiled, and thanked him.

He looked at me and said, "Always hold your head up high and be proud of who you are. The imagination is a powerful thing. Only you could see and hear me. No one else could. You did those amazing things because you believed in me and my God. Never stop believing, Little Sam. Never stop believing. Believe in yourself and all the possibilities of what you can do with my God, the True and Living God, on your side. Never sell out your God who gave you the power to do all those incredible things. That's where I made my mistake. Many times, I did things God told me not to do, and I suffered greatly for it. I was betrayed by the woman I loved because of my disobedience. I took life and things for granted because of my strength. I was the strongest man of my times until they cut my hair. Then I was caught and bound like any human and had my eyes put out. I was treated worse than an animal. I don't want that to happen to you, Little Sam. My whole life was taken away from me in a matter of minutes, but you know what?"

I sat there spellbound, listening to him, and said, "What, Samson?"

"My God never left me alone. He allowed my hair to grow back, and I regained my strength. I couldn't see, but I could hear the crowd above me. I had the young boy that led me by the hand to stand me between two pillars of the house, so I could feel them."

He began flexing his arms, and his sadness turned to joy, and his countenance changed.

He said, "My God gave me victory that day. There were three thousand men and women there, plus lords of the Philistines. I pushed against those pillars so hard until I brought that place down. I destroyed those Philistines and lost my life in the process, but God had restored my strength. I knew he had not forgotten about me. Little Sam, he will always be there for you when you obey and believe."

"I believe, Samson. I believe," I said.

He was so amazing. I couldn't help but take a deep breath from listening to him. The more he spoke, the more I wanted to be like him. There was no one in the world like Samson.

He said, "I am so proud that I had this time with you. Never take life and people for granted, Little Sam— never. You will always suffer the consequences of your actions just as I did. Obey your parents and your God so you can live a long time on this earth."

He wiped the tears from his eyes, and I wiped some from mine. He went on his way with me waving until he was out of sight.

The next thing I knew, my daddy was waking me up.

"Get up, Samson. Let's get ready to go. We have a lot to do in town today."

I thought I was already awake. I pulled myself together, jumped up with excitement, and put on my clothes. Daddy and I quickly ate our breakfast and headed for the truck. I was ready to discover who was behind this land-grabbing scheme.

Driving into town, Daddy appeared to be a little nervous. I asked him to slow down when he began to zigzag in the road.

"Are you okay, Daddy?" I asked.

He said, "I'm okay, but this is really something, Samson. I never thought anything like this could happen to us. Son, we are going to be very rich, and I don't know how to take this right now."

"Daddy, you are going to be just fine after all of this is over. Just wait and see." I continued to talk, and soon, he began to relax.

He drove on down the road a piece and then suddenly stopped the truck on the side of the road. I didn't know what was going on. He looked at me strangely, got out of the truck, smiled, and then laughed out real loud as hard as he could. This was weird for my daddy because he was usually so predictable. I couldn't help but laugh with him.

He said, "Samson, you can stick your head out the truck and let your hair blow in the wind all you want. I don't care anymore. Let it grow as long as you want. I am so grateful to have you as my son. You are no ordinary young man. You are extraordinary with a capital E," and he laughed some more.

I smiled and gave him a big hug. He looked toward the North Creek area. Then he looked at me like he had an amazing thought in his head.

He said, "Samson, guess what?"

I said, "What, Daddy?"

"I think we are going to build us a resort when this is over. Those land robbers did us a favor by going ahead and marking off the land. I couldn't have done it better myself. Thanks to you, we have all the plans in our possession. I have never seen such a beautiful place before in all my life. That storm really did us good. What do you think about that?"

I jumped up, smiled, and said, "It sure sounds good to me, Daddy," and we got back in the truck.

CHAPTER 20

I Smell a Rat

WE FINALLY ARRIVED IN TOWN, AND DADDY PULLED up to the sheriff's office. I could feel the tension in the air. Daddy asked me to come in with him just in case the sheriff had some questions for me. We went in, and the sheriff asked us to have a seat.

He said, "How are you doing there, Mr. Avery?"

"Fine, Sheriff. Just fine. Can't wait for all this to be over."

The sheriff yawned and said, "I think we are about ready to crack this case. We found a lot of evidence in that helicopter wreckage. You will be surprised to know that some key people in this town are involved in it. That helicopter is the one the mayor uses when traveling out of town."

When he said that, boy, I got all excited. I just knew

it was the mayor. Even in all that dust, I thought I recognized him.

The sheriff arose from his chair and said, "We'll be going over to the mayor's office as soon as the FBI arrive."

Deep down in my gut, I could smell a big rat. I knew the mayor had something to do with it, but why? *He's got to be that Mr. Big,* I thought.

While we were waiting in the sheriff's office for the FBI to arrive, the door opened. Several deputies brought in some of those men who were hurt in the helicopter crash. Just as I expected, they were all limping. Some were wearing bandages, but they all had on handcuffs. The deputies proudly put them all behind bars.

One of the men behind bars yelled out to my daddy, "You are a dead man, Mr. Avery. You will never enjoy that land or that oil. You better watch your step because your end is closer than you think!"

Daddy was shocked. He didn't know what to say or do. He was terrified. He had never, ever caused anyone any trouble in Soyerville. Now, someone wanted to hurt him. I could see the fear in his face.

He turned to the sheriff and said, "What did that man mean by that? What's going on?"

Daddy had never seen that man a day in his life. Soyerville is a very small town, and he knew just about everyone. He couldn't understand why he would say something like that.

The sheriff told my daddy, "This man is one of the men that were trying to steal your cattle and land. He knows more than he's telling us. Don't you worry now, Mr. Avery. We are closing in on them."

Another one of the men behind bars yelled, "Hey, you, kid with the long hair. We are going to get you too. You have been nothing but trouble for us."

He just didn't know how ready I was for them. I couldn't wait for the FBI to get there so I could start looking around. Impatiently, I sat at a table playing checkers with one of the deputies.

The FBI finally arrived, and we all prepared to go over to the mayor's office. I was eager to go with them. Daddy turned and looked at me. He told me to go on over to the burger shop and get me a burger or something instead. He felt I would probably get in the way or even get hurt. He reached into his pocket and pulled out a $20 bill and gave it to me.

I went off with a very empty stomach. Suddenly, this strange feeling came over me as if there was going to be trouble. I mean big trouble.

I went on into the burger shop. To my surprise, Cynthia was there, eating. I couldn't believe it. I was so glad to see her. I went over and asked if I could sit with her. She smiled and said I could. The waitress came over and smiled.

"So, what are you going to have this time?"

I looked at her and smiled. "Five giant burgers with three large orders of fries, four giant sodas, and three big slices of cake with two scoops of ice cream on top of each one this time."

The waitress looked at me in shock and said, "Now, you just got to be kidding me, right?"

I said, "Oh no, I'm really hungry this time."

I must admit looking into Cynthia's beautiful brown eyes increased my appetite even more. *I sure hope she doesn't think I'm abnormal,* I thought.

"Cynthia, please forgive me today. I'm so hungry I could eat a horse," I said.

She sat there in awe and said, "Samson, I want to see you eat that horse," and then she started smiling.

I said, "I'm going to give it my best shot."

The room became silent for a minute. The waitress alerted some of the people in the diner, and the bets were on again, as I was hoping they would be. Now $300 was on the table. Cynthia was very impressed.

Someone said, "No way he can eat all that food."

That created even more excitement. Everyone watched, including Cynthia, as the waitress set my food on the table. I whispered a prayer to Samson's God to help me. I ate, and ate, and ate. In no time, everything was gone.

Various people were saying, "I just can't believe it." "That's humanly impossible." "No one can eat like that."

"It should be against the law to eat that much." "His stomach is like a bottomless pit."

Bottomless pit or not, I was $300 richer. I said goodbye to Cynthia and everyone else and left.

While leaving the burger shop, I felt myself swelling up again and feeling strange. I turned to look down the street toward the sheriff's office and saw the people gathering there. The sheriff and my daddy were standing in the middle of the street with several other people. I didn't know if they were going to the mayor's office or returning from it.

Walking back to the sheriff's office to meet my daddy, I noticed three men from the diner were following me. I quickly ducked into the alley to get away from them. One man had a stick, and another one had a chain. I guessed they wanted to beat me up and take my money. Suddenly, I started swelling and growing. I don't know what those men saw, but they took off running and ran into the wall and knocked themselves out. I left them out cold and went to meet my daddy.

While on my way to the sheriff's office, I was soon shaken by a huge explosion. All I could see were people running for cover. It was pure pandemonium. Everyone ran down the street to see what was going on.

I ran as fast as I could to make sure my daddy was all right. I got there in a matter of seconds. It was unbelievable. It appeared an abandoned warehouse had been blown to smithereens for some reason. Something like this had never happened before in Soyerville, so why now?

The sheriff cried out, "What in the world is going on? This is strange. The warehouse blew up!"

Thank goodness no one was seriously injured in the blast. Horribly, there was extensive damage to several nearby buildings.

Everyone brushed themselves off and headed over to the mayor's office as planned. I looked for my daddy in the crowd, but he was gone. He was standing right over there a minute ago, and now he was gone. When the crowd moved, he suddenly disappeared. He was nowhere. I called to him, trying to look over the crowd.

"Daddy! Daddy, where are you?" There was no answer.

I asked the sheriff, "Sheriff, where is my daddy? Where is he? You were supposed to protect him."

He said, "Who is your daddy, son? I don't recognize you. Tell me his name."

What's going on? I thought. The sheriff didn't recognize me.

I said in distress, "I'm Samson. Sheriff, don't you recognize me?"

He said, "Samson who, son? I only know one Samson, and that's Samson Avery, and you are not him."

Amid all the confusion, I heard Samson's voice say, "They will not recognize you."

I had to see who the sheriff was looking at. I went over to the window and couldn't believe who I saw. It was the guy with all the muscles who had followed me—the one I had seen in the mirror that time but never found. I laughed at the thought of me chasing my own tail. I looked just like Samson, but in a different time. I had on my same clothes, and muscles like I had never seen on me before.

I began looking through the crowd for my daddy. He was gone. I was getting angrier by the second. I wanted to tear up the whole town and find him.

Suddenly, the building next to city hall blew up. All the people on the street scattered, trying to take cover. That caused even more confusion.

Someone yelled, "Sheriff, the mayor went into that building over there a little while ago. We need to check and make sure that he's all right."

The town was now in a panic, wondering what was going on. The people were all terrified.

The sheriff yelled, "Keep the women and children away from this place! It's not safe."

The fire department was putting out the fire from the first explosion, and now, this building was on fire.

"The Honorable Mayor is probably dead by now, Sheriff," someone said.

I kept thinking this just didn't make any sense. My daddy disappeared, and now the mayor was dead? The

FBI was on the phone, calling for backup. I couldn't understand the mayor dying in the explosion if he was Mr. Big, or my daddy disappearing if they didn't need him. Somebody needed my daddy alive, but who?

CHAPTER 21

Bringing Down the Philistines

WHEN I THOUGHT THINGS WERE ABOUT TO CALM down, another explosion happened not far from the last explosion. Three explosions back to back. It was like a war zone in this quiet town of Soyerville. This time, several people were injured because they took cover near the explosion site before it happened.

Now, I was mad. Attention had shifted from going to find the mayor to finding my daddy, to tending to the injured from the explosions, to putting out fires. If that wasn't strange, I didn't know what was. This all seemed planned to me, and my daddy was drawn into it.

I remembered what that prisoner said: "You are a dead man, Mr. Avery." I knew he wasn't dead. Someone was going through too much trouble to scare everyone.

It took several hours for the sheriff to get things under control. He told the people not to worry because they were going to find my daddy and those behind this horrible crime. I stood by, watching as the sheriff and the FBI headed back over to the mayor's office.

Someone fired a shot from an upstairs window, and everyone scrambled to take cover. I heard the sheriff angrily say, "What in the world is going on around here? Will somebody please tell me?"

Enough was enough, and I decided to do my own detective work, whoever I was at the time. I left the group and went in search of my daddy. I went into a nearby building and out the back door. I went up nearly two blocks, turned the corner, and crossed the street where no one could see me. I went to the back of the building where the shots were fired.

Someone fired another shot, and the sheriff returned fire. In all the chaos, a couple of officers had been shot. I heard the sheriff telling everyone to stay down and out of sight. These folks were aiming to kill, and people were getting shot. I was really scared for my daddy. *Who has my daddy, and where did they take him?* That was all I could think about. That Mr. Big had probably planned the whole thing. He wanted my daddy out of the way so he could get our land.

I finally made my way up the side of the building to an open window. I pulled off the screen, climbed in, and quietly made my way to the room where the shots were coming from. Peeping through the window, I could see several men were in there. I went into the room next to it and looked out the window to see what I could see. They had a clear shot of the sheriff's office. In fact, they had a good view of that whole side of the street. These uncircumcised Philistines had come to the end of the road.

Suddenly, something came over me. I turned and headed to the room where the men were. I had this surge of energy and burst into the room, catching the men off guard. I knocked all three of them out with a single punch. I tied them up, gagged them, and hung them from the window for everyone to see who they were. They were men who worked in the mayor's office.

I slowly made my way to the mayor's office as the FBI and the sheriff entered the building. To my surprise, the mayor had booby-trapped his whole wing. *Why would he do that?* I took one step, and a bell went off. I was so scared. I didn't know what was going to happen at that point. I took another step.

Then I heard someone say, "Come any closer, and this building will go up in flames."

I didn't know what to do then. I stopped in my tracks.

Then he said, "I'm not going to prison for anyone. That nosy kid messed up everything, and somebody's going to pay. I've got your Mr. Avery. If you want him alive, you better stay back and listen to what I have to say."

My daddy was alive. That was all I needed to know.

The FBI and the sheriff arrived on the floor with their guns drawn. I saw them in the mirror on the wall. I slowly backed away so they couldn't see me and yelled, "The floor is booby-trapped, Sheriff! They have Mr. Avery in there." I also told them what the man said.

The sheriff said, "Thank you. Now hurry and get out. It's too dangerous for anyone to be up here."

In my heart, I knew I was not leaving without my daddy. The sheriff called out to the man and told him to surrender. The man told them that he would die first and take everyone with him.

The sheriff recognized his voice and said, "That's the mayor talking. I can't believe this. What in the world is going on?" He yelled out, "Don't be crazy, Mr. Mayor! You are supposed to protect the people, not destroy them and the town."

The mayor said angrily, "I will blow up you and this whole town if I have to."

It startled me when someone suddenly tapped me on the shoulder. I turned around and was surprised to see that it was Samson. I thought he had left me forever. I was so glad to see him. He asked me to quietly follow him. I left with him to see what he wanted. The fight was now on for sure, because Samson was here.

He said, "I need you to trust my God and your gut, Little Sam. This is going to be a tough one. Trust your gut."

I had a feeling the mayor was bluffing. I was going to trust my gut on that.

I remembered how Samson brought down that house with the three-thousand-plus people before he died in the Bible. I certainly wasn't ready to die, but I went outside and took a good look at the building from the back side. Suddenly, I started bulking up again. I called on Samson's God, and I began pushing up against that building the mayor was in. The building began to rock.

People on the inside were screaming, "Earthquake! Earthquake!" and started running out.

Samson appeared to help me out. We shook that building like it had never been shaken before. It felt good! Bricks fell from everywhere.

The sheriff, the FBI agents, and those with them ran out of the building in a panic. They thought it was probably some sort of aftershock from the explosions.

The mayor was so scared that he forgot he was the villain. He came rushing out of the building, hopping on his crutches. He had no place for his weapon because he needed both hands for the crutches. Very scared and disgusted, he yelled a few curse words and surrendered without a fight. We really called his bluff. However, there was still no sight of my daddy. *Where is he?* was all I could ask myself.

I quickly went back into that building to find my daddy. I called repeatedly out to him. "Daddy! Daddy, where are you?"

I heard a faint, muffled sound come from a back corner in one of the rooms and went looking for him. They had left him there tied up in a corner with tape over his mouth. There was no way for him to get loose. He could have died if there had been an actual earthquake.

Apparently, I was back to normal because he recognized me. He said, "Samson, I am so glad to see you."

I untied him, gave him a big hug, and prepared to take him out of the building. He felt he had a fractured rib and a broken toe. He was absolutely traumatized.

He said, "Son, that earthquake nearly scared me to death. I didn't know what I was going to do." He gave me a big hug again and said, "I didn't want to die without seeing you. My big, old trouble maker."

I slowly brought Daddy down from the building because of his injuries, and we joined the others. We all went back over to the sheriff's office. Daddy wanted to wrap up the investigation first before he went to the doctor.

Unexpectedly, we heard this loud, rumbling noise and went back outside to see what it was. Just like that, the mayor's building tumbled down to the ground. For a few minutes, we were all blinded by the dust from it and in total shock. I guess Samson and I shook that building harder than we intended. I could now see how that house came down and killed all those Philistines.

The sheriff said, "Samson, now that was close. Another minute, and you and your daddy would have gotten caught in that. Looks like you do have an angel watching over you after all, Mr. Avery."

Daddy said, "That I do, Sheriff. That I do." He looked at me with a great big smile on his face.

I looked over to the side of the building and saw Samson waving at me. I was so excited to see him. I told Daddy I had left something on the side of the building and needed to go get it. I left them to go say goodbye to Samson. As hard as it was, I waved back. I knew he was leaving me for good. I couldn't let him go without personally thanking him once more.

He smiled and said, "We did it, didn't we, Little Sam? We brought those uncircumcised Philistines down. Now your family and all your neighbors can enjoy their land."

I smiled, gave him a big hug with tears in my eyes, and said, "We sure did, and shook that building down to. That was so awesome!"

"It sure was, Little Sam," he said, holding back his tears. "I'm going to have to go now. I want you to remember everything I taught you. You never know, I just might show up again one day."

I looked at him with tears in my eyes and said, "Thank you for everything, Samson. I'm really going to miss you. You are the best friend I ever had." *I sure wish you could stay*, I said to myself.

He walked away like a giant and began to slowly fade from my sight. I had a big lump in my throat as I waved goodbye to him.

I heard him say, "See you around, Little Sam. See you around," as his laugh vanished like an echo in the air.

Sadly, I walked on back to the sheriff's office.

Daddy looked at me strangely and said, "Who were you waving at, son?"

I smiled and said, "The one who helped us, Daddy. The one who helped us."

While walking to the truck, Daddy looked at me and said, "Are you okay, son? You just don't look right. Is it because you thought you had lost me?"

"Daddy," I said, "you just don't know how scared I was for you. If anything had happened to you, I don't know what I would have done. I was not going to leave that building until I found you. To think the mayor would do something like that to you makes me so angry. He was supposed to be your best friend. He knew just about everything about us."

"I know, son," Daddy said. "Greed has always been the thing that drives a wedge between friends. The mayor had asked me a few questions about the North

Creek area several times, but I never caught on to why. I trusted him a little too much. This has really taught me a lesson. I am so grateful to God for you. I love you so much."

"I love you too, Daddy," I said.

He put his hand on my head and wiggled my hair while I was sitting on a stump and said, "I just don't know what I would have done if something had happened to you."

I said, "I know, Daddy. To think we made it safely out of that building in the nick of time was a miracle. I know God had someone looking out for us."

Daddy said, "Yes, one of his angels, and his name is Samson."

I looked at my daddy, puzzled. Did he know that it was the real Samson, and not me? I realized he didn't know when he said, "Thank you so much, son, for saving my life. Had it not been for you, the mayor would have all our land today. I'm so glad he didn't ask me to sign anything. You are my hero."

He wiped the tears from his eyes and said, "Now let's get in the truck and go home."

I said, "Yes sir. I sure hope Mama cooked a good dinner."

He tossed me the keys and said, "Samson, you drive this time. My ribs and toe are hurting me a little."

I was sorry for his pain, but I felt like the cow that

jumped over the moon when he asked me to drive. I was so excited. No more pedal cars for me. I had finally moved up to the big truck! I took my ponytail down and let my hair blow in the wind.

He laughed at me and said, "Yes, son, let it blow! Let's go home and see what your mama cooked."

Driving off, I couldn't help but think about Samson, the one who helped make me a hero in my daddy's eyes.

CHAPTER 22

A Happy Ending

AFTER ALL THE ACTION IN TOWN, DADDY AND I drove along the highway, laughing and talking about all the things that had happened to us. It was almost like something we had seen on television, except we were the characters in it. That was soon interrupted. Whatever Mama was cooking suddenly attacked our noses and held us hostage as we drove home. That smell settled right inside the truck. Daddy and I, like detectives, tried to decipher what Mama was cooking from the smell.

I sniffed like a puppy dog and said, "Barbeque with baked beans, corn on the cob, and Texas toast."

Daddy said, "No, I believe it's a delicious beef roast with the trimmings, cabbage, and sweet potato pie."

I laughed hysterically and said, "I don't know about that, Daddy."

He smiled and said, "I'm sticking to my guns on this one. It sure smells like a delicious beef roast with the trimmings, cabbage, and sweet potato pie," to me.

I laughed and said, "I'm willing to bet you it's not."

He looked at me, frowned, and said, "All right then, big man, how much do you want to bet?"

Remembering Samson, I decided to trust my gut. I said teasingly, "What about a million dollars?"

Daddy bucked his eyes, leaned his head back, and looked at me like I was crazy. I was only kidding at the time, but for some reason, Daddy took me very seriously.

He smiled and said, "All right, if I win, I expect you to pay up now."

I looked at him, smiled, and said, "Yes, sir."

The truth is, I only had $300 to my name. That was what I had won at the diner. We both laughed, and I drove on home.

I slowly pulled the truck into the shed, and we got out. Daddy patted me on the back and said, "Good job, son. If you keep driving like this, I just might let you drive by yourself one day."

I couldn't hold back the smiles.

We went in the house and gave Mama a big hug. She looked at me and said, "Now, what are you all smiles about? I haven't seen that many teeth in a while."

"Daddy said I did good driving home, and one day I can drive the truck by myself."

"Oh, he did, did he? That's wonderful. Now go on and wash up so you can eat dinner."

She noticed Daddy was limping. You would have thought the world was coming to an end the way she was acting. I can't remember anything bad ever happening to him in my life. She was devastated.

"Oh my Lord! Honey, what happened? Why are you limping? Do you need to go to the doctor? Come on and sit down over here."

She grabbed him around his waist to help him to the chair, and he grunted. That really did it.

"You have broken bones? Y'all better tell me what happened right now."

Daddy finally calmed her down. He told her that he was okay and what happened to us in town. She couldn't believe it. All she could say was, "Oh my Lord!"

Daddy asked her if we could eat because he was starving. She began putting the food on the table. She had done it again. The house smelled so good. I couldn't wait to eat.

Looking at the table, I realized trusting my gut had failed me miserably. I don't know how Daddy knew, but Mama had cooked a beautiful beef roast with all the trimmings; cabbage, corn, sweet potato pie, corn bread, and iced tea were on the table. I felt sick to my stomach.

Mama looked at me very concerned and said, "Are you okay, Samson? You don't look so good."

I sadly looked at my daddy, and he looked at me and burst out laughing, holding his side. I was still wondering, *How in the world did he know what Mama was cooking?*

"Now what's going on with you two?" Mama asked.

Daddy laughed and said, "It's okay, Samson. You are my son. What you did today clears all your debt. You don't owe me anything. You saved my life."

That was a big relief. Now, I could breathe again. He told Mama that I had bet him a million dollars that we were not having beef roast for dinner. Mama looked at me, shook her head, and smiled.

He said, "Son, let this be a lesson to you. Never bet what you don't have. In fact, never bet at all. I asked your mama to fix beef roast for dinner today, and she did. Honey, thank you so much."

In that moment, I realized that one day, I was going to be a very rich man. After that experience, I didn't think I would ever want to make another bet—not even kidding. I almost lost a million dollars just like that.

CHAPTER 23

A Brand-New Start

FOUR YEARS LATER

SOYERVILLE HAS ALWAYS BEEN A VERY QUIET little place and never had so much action. People are still trying to figure out what happened. The mayor and his group have all gone to federal prison for a very long time. Part of the town is still in shambles from the explosions.

At the time, little did we know we had made history that day. "Bombs, Bullets and Bad Men" was our newspaper and local television headline. It being such a small town, we never expected to catch the attention of other newspapers and television stations across the country.

Some movie company showed up wanting to get the

rights to do a movie about us. The company even asked me to be in it. I was going to be a real movie star. The funny thing is one of those big shampoo companies saw my picture on the news. The company was so impressed with my hair that company representatives came all the way down to Soyerville. They asked me to do a shampoo commercial. That was the first time I ever saw myself in action on television. Later, that company sent me a big bonus check because it sold so much shampoo that year.

After doing the commercial, my whole life changed. I had never had so many girls wanting to talk to me and asking for my telephone number before in my life. Now, that didn't sit well with Cynthia at all. Even though she gets jealous sometimes, she is still my Delilah, and the only girl for me.

Someone took pictures of the city for historical purposes before rebuilding began. "It's good to be able to look back and compare the old Soyerville with the new one in the future," he said.

The most exciting part of this story is the town honored me as the youngest hero for saving my daddy's and all the neighbors' property, telling them about the North Creek area, and stopping the corruption that was coming out of the mayor's office. The town presented me with a plaque with a few words on it that I will always treasure. In big gold letters, it read, "SAMSON,

No Ordinary Superhero. You are an extraordinary one!" I felt like a giant among men.

I couldn't tell the people who the real hero was: my friend Samson, the strongest man in the Bible. They would have thought I was crazy and locked me up for good. I will always cherish his memory and our great times spent together, even if most of those times happened in my dreams.

Looking back, nearly four years later, I believe Soyerville is a most beautiful town after its restoration and fame. All the buildings have been rebuilt with some of Daddy's oil money. The town added a movie theater, a bigger hospital, a new elementary school and high school, a grand hotel, a larger family restaurant, a public library, a swimming pool, and so much more.

The town elected a new mayor and other public officials. They wanted to make my daddy mayor, but he politely turned them down. He said it was going to take him a long while to get over what had happened to him.

It turned out that it was the mayor who discovered the oil on our property. Daddy had given him permission to fish and hunt there anytime he pleased. He must have discovered the oil when he went to get water from one of those wells. Samson was right when he said, "Trust no one, no matter how well you think you know them. Be cautious and be very careful. Many times, it will be those people that will betray you or even kill you." Who would have ever thought the man my father went to school with, sat on the board with, had dinner at our house with many times, and hunted with would betray him like that?

Daddy got all the rights to his oil and made sure he still had his land. He even gave money to all the neighbors who had lost their cattle to buy more cattle and whatever else they needed. They were so grateful to my daddy. The neighbors even went in together and built their own meat-processing plant and grocery store. Now that was amazing.

Mama and Daddy are now living it up, being rich. We have taken several great vacations across the United States and out of the country. Daddy even had her a new house built with one of those great big kitchens like you see on television. He even got someone to cook for her. It's funny seeing Mama and the cook clashing because Mama wants to always tell her how to cook. I discovered that the cook soon figured out that if she wanted to keep her job, she had to cook like Mama wanted her to. I must say she has gotten pretty good at it.

Daddy has a limo now and someone to drive it for him. My daddy has never smoked a day in his life. Now, he keeps Cuban cigars in his limo.

Life has truly been amazing for all of us, now being rich. It's a side of life I could have never imagined. Who would have ever thought something like this could happen to people like us living in the sticks of Soyerville?

The oil wells are pumping thousands of gallons of oil a day. I never imagined seeing the construction of oil wells with my very own eyes. They are awesome.

The Samson Avery Resort is open and brings in thousands of people each week. The mayor's designs for the place worked out perfectly. Samson and I found the designs and fake permits to build on our property in a briefcase along with a lot of cash. We found that stuff not far from that helicopter wreckage. I guess the mayor thought it was all destroyed in the fire.

As for me, my hair is still growing. I get it cut a few inches at a time. Cynthia and I are enjoying more than studying together. She loves combing my hair and trying to figure out my riddles. Sometimes, I test her to see if she tells anyone. So far, she hasn't told a soul.

Samson gave me a great appreciation for reading the Bible. I never thought a book like that could become so real in my life. It brought out all my inner strength and courage that I didn't even know I had. I'm looking forward to going on another great adventure, if not with Samson again, perhaps with another Bible legend. I've been reading 1 Samuel, and I came upon a boy named David. He was a shepherd boy, and Samuel anointed his head with oil to be the king of Israel one day. At this point, I've had no contact with this character.

I must have fallen asleep because I felt someone shaking me and saying, "Samson! Samson wake up."

When I open my eyes, it was Mama. She was waking me up so I could start packing to go on vacation.

She said, "I heard you talking in your sleep. You were saying something about Samson and your children. It sure must have been a good dream, because you don't have any children, yet."

I became so excited when she said that. I quickly jump out of the bed and put on my clothes. I went outside and walk down by the creek. I sat down under that big old oak tree where it all started. All I could think about was Samson all over again.

I must have fallen asleep again because I saw myself teaching my children about the Bible. We were having so much fun. Suddenly, Samson tiptoed into the room. He placed one finger over his mouth looking at me. He smiled and asked my children to follow him. He waved goodbye to me, and out the door they went.

Sadly, I looked out the window with tearful eyes. I watched them as they laughed with him. They jumped over cliffs and streams with him the same way I used to. And just like that, they slowly vanished from my sight.

Then, I heard Samson say excitedly, "See you later, Little Sam," as his voice echoed through the air, and slowly faded away.

Printed in the United States
By Bookmasters